JAKE LOGAN

SLOCUM AND THE DEATH DEALER

D1562298

B

BERKLEY BOOKS, NEW YORK

SLOCUM AND THE DEATH DEALER

A Berkley Book / published by arrangement with
the author

PRINTING HISTORY
Berkley edition / February 1991

ISBN: 0-425-12558-0

A BERKLEY BOOK ® TM 757,375
Berkley Books are published by The Berkley Publishing Group,
200 Madison Avenue, New York, New York 10016.
The name "BERKLEY" and the "B" logo
are trademarks belonging to Berkley Publishing Corporation.

PRINTED IN THE UNITED STATES OF AMERICA

10 9 8 7 6 5 4 3 2 1

SLOCUM AND THE
DEATH DEALER

1

Slocum had been feeling good before he reached Bill Selby's ranch. That was fate—it slipped you a taste of honey before it kicked you in the gut.

Earlier that day, he'd crossed a parched trail and stopped in the Five Spots saloon to cut the dust with a few snorts. Then he had a feverish tangle with a saloon tart, unsuitably named Velvet, who bucked on the bed like a mare on a red-hot griddle. Afterward, he had a fine dinner of steak, yams, and okra at Mama Joy's Cafe. When he started for Selby's ranch, four miles past the town of Five Spots, he felt mighty good. Then he ran straight into misery.

First, it was Bill's ranch house, looking like it had been gutted by a Comanche mob. Then three bullets whistled past him, almost blowing his head off, forcing him to jump from the roan and crawl into the bushes. The bullets came from dense shrubs west of the house, from one gun. At least he didn't face a bunch.

Who the hell could it be?

Silently, Slocum shifted his position and stroked his chin. Whenever he passed through southern Texas, he made a point to visit Bill Selby, a hell of a brave sidekick. They had enlisted together in Calhoun County, and had fought part of the bloody war as comrades. After the war, Bill went through hard times, but it seemed he had straightened out and bought the ranch in Five Spots.

Slocum, from behind the cover of thick shrubs, stared at the house, blackened by fire. Who did it? Comanche renegades, out to steal? Greedy drifters? Outlaws?

And what about Bill and his two sons, the oldest, Tad, a stripling, and that impish, smiling kid, Seth? Bill had lost his wife with the birth of Seth, five years ago.

Slocum's jaw hardened; he had to get behind the bush-whacker lurking in the brush. Slocum knew the terrain; he crawled silently, circled behind the thick shrubs and brush with the stealth of an Indian, and before long he had the shooter in his sights. No Comanche, no drifter— just a young gunman holding a pistol and trying to figure his next move.

"Drop the gun." Slocum's voice was curt.

The gunman jumped, then turned and tried to shoot. Slocum shot the pistol out of his hand.

Slocum came forward, and, for the first time, got a clear look; a yearling with a square, honest face, and clear blue eyes like those of Bill Selby. It was Tad, Bill's firstborn.

Slocum came close.

"What the hell, you trying to kill me, Tad?"

The stripling was startled. "Mr. Slocum? Is it you?"

"Yeah, it's me, and you almost put me in Boot Hill."

Tad groaned. "God." He rubbed a hand over his face, as

if trying to wipe out a terrible memory. "I didn't know. I thought it was them. God, Slocum, it's bad."

Slocum felt evil foreboding.

Tad glanced toward the house and pain gleamed in his eyes. He bit his lip, trying valiantly to play the man in the face of something terrible.

Slocum's voice was taut. "What is it? Where's your dad?"

A sharp intake of breath, then Tad's voice cracked. "He's dead. Seth is dead, too. They shot dad to pieces. The house is ransacked, burned." His eyes welled with tears. He was just a stripling.

Slocum felt a rush of sorrow. Bill Selby, true-blue, a fun-loving, loyal sidekick in the bad days of the war, dead. And his son, Seth, a laughing, clear-eyed kid full of the joy of life. Slocum felt the threat of life's brevity, then the deep burn of anger.

"Who did it?"

"Don't know. I stayed at the Bill Davis ranch last night. And came home to this. Dad, shot to pieces. And my little brother, Seth." His voice broke. "When I saw you, I was loco, didn't look, figgered you were with those who did the massacre. So I started to shoot." Tad ran his hand through his honey-colored hair.

"It's bad, Slocum." He started for the house, but stopped outside. He'd seen the carnage.

Inside, Slocum smelled the acrid odor of burnt wood; the place was a shambles, a pitiful sight. Bill, his strong face distorted with agony, lay hog-tied, with eight bullets in his bloody body. The killers had taken no chances. His holster was empty; they had lifted his gun, tied him, and killed in cold blood. Seth, the boy, with his long yellow hair, lay sprawled on the floor. Why'd they kill the kid?

No witnesses? And there was another corpse—a stranger. Tad told Slocum he had never seen the man before. Drawers were turned out, a strongbox shot open. Robbery. Bill Selby was not a poor man.

Slocum's teeth clenched as he came out of the house and examined the prints. Six booted men, not Comanches. He noticed the prints of seven horses. One must have belonged to the mysterious dead man.

Tad, his face dark with anger, was silent as they dug the graves. Then he looked up at the sky; gray, lowering, threatening rain.

Two buzzards floated high. The smell of death always brought them. In sudden fury, Tad grabbed his gun and fired, but his bullets did nothing to their patient circling.

Slocum looked at the kid's sullen, tear-stained face.

Tad was breathing deeply. "Before God, I swear, I'll follow those tracks, find those dogs, and kill 'em or get killed. I swear it."

Slocum clenched his teeth. It was not the first time he'd heard such vows, but never so fiercely spoken. Tad burned with a terrible thirst for revenge. But he'd face five brutal thieves, professional killers, not the kind a stripling could handle.

Slocum remembered Bill Selby, his loyal comrade in the good times and the bad ones. He, too, felt the rage. Killers had come out of nowhere to brutally murder Bill. And Seth, a laughing, innocent kid, cut down before he started living. The scum who did it had to pay.

"We'll do it together, Tad," he said.

Tad turned, his eyes flooded with tears. He moved close to Slocum who put a hand on his shoulder.

Later, Slocum studied the prints. "Maybe they're headed

for Red Creek. Got to stop somewhere. We'll find them."

They started to ride. Slocum glanced at the sky, still bloated with gray clouds; in the distance, the bronze mountains sprawled, massively indifferent. Tad rode silently, looking fiercely ahead.

The powerful roan moved smoothly under Slocum. Something was odd about these killings. Was it cold-blooded massacre and plundering? Or something else? Where did the mysterious dead man fit into the picture? Why was the kid slaughtered in front of his father—almost like a sacrificial lamb, as if to give him more pain than death? Was it to pressure Bill to reveal his money? Did he have money? Lots of money? How did they know? The answer lay out there, with the killers.

After three hours of riding, following the tracks toward Red Creek, they stopped for beef jerky and coffee, and to let the horses drink.

The sky, still bloated with clouds, made Slocum uneasy. The outlaws seemed to be headed for Red Creek, but there was no guarantee, and if rain came, it might erase the tracks. That'd be bad.

Tad was silent, his jaw clenched, his blue eyes still dazed, as if he hadn't yet digested the terror of suddenly being stripped of his family. Slocum felt his sorrow.

Finally Tad spoke, his voice querulous. "Why'd they do it, Slocum?"

Slocum stroked his chin. "Did your father have a lot of money, Tad?"

"I reckon he had some. Never seemed short. Always got what he wanted. He bought and sold stock. Yes, I figure he had money."

"Money is like dead meat, attracts buzzards," Slocum said.

"But the way they killed him. They hog-tied him. My father. He was the most decent man I ever knew. Why? And they killed Seth, just a kid. And what about that other one? Who was he? Why?"

"They're scum, that's why. Who can explain it, Tad?"

"They killed Seth, right in front of him. Why'd they do that?"

That was the mystery, Slocum thought. They not only wanted to rob Selby, but give him lots of pain. There had to be reasons.

Tad grimaced. "Too bad I wasn't there to help."

Privately, Slocum thought that was a good thing; they'd have struck him down, too. "They were killers, Tad. They wanted to hurt your father. Maybe that mattered more than the money."

"Well, mebbe they're riding to Red Creek. We gotta find 'em." The jaw in his strong young face hardened. "*Gotta.*"

They could be riding to Red Creek or to Aurora, depending on the trail they took at the fork. The trouble was that heavy rain clouds were scudding across the sky, and a west wind was gusting hard.

"We better get goin'," Slocum said.

Twenty minutes later, the rain came down in buckets, and lasted half an hour. It left the earth soggy and trackless.

They took shelter in a rock cave, and when the rain clouds swept by, they rode again. A hard, pushing wind cleared the sky overhead and a glowing sun began to dry the earth.

The land on the west was broken by hollows, folded hills,

and serrated mountains. They rode the trail silently through grassy land until they came to the road fork. Which trail to take? They had no tracks to work with. One led to Red Creek, the other to Aurora.

Where would such a gang go? They had money and would want to spend it. Or would they lay low? Not a chance, such killers used guns ruthlessly. Cleverly, too, because they caught Bill Selby off guard, didn't they? He wondered if they knew about Tad.

"Did your dad have an enemy? Did he have a fight with someone?"

Tad shook his head. "Folks liked him. You knew dad. He enjoyed a laugh. He was straight and honest. Why'd they come to kill him?"

Slocum rubbed his jaw. "Mighty strange. Someone knew about his money. Someone in the territory. You keep thinking about it. Maybe you'll remember."

Tad shook his head. "No. There was nobody. How do *you* figure it?"

"Hard to say." Slocum stared west at the soaring mountains. "I told you. Gunmen prowling. They coulda heard your dad had a fine ranch and moseyed up to grab what they could."

Tad rubbed his smooth cheek vigorously, as if he had an ache and hoped to rub it away. "But it don't matter. Blood for blood." He stared at the trail. "Which way?"

Slocum swung into his saddle, his face lean, weathered, grim. Thieves and killers were running free and, in this land, your gun was the law. If the scum took over, the land would become a gathering place for ruffians, unsafe for women, kids, men of goodwill. A man needed to stand up, to clean out the rotten coyotes who, more and more, cluttered the territory. There were men out there who needed killing, so that boys like Tad would not live with a burden of sorrow from losing kin.

"Let's go to Red Creek." Slocum figured it was a tough town where a gang of killers would feel easy.

2

Just before sundown, they reached Red Creek, which nestled in the hills just two miles from the border. Four sleazy denizens of the town, lounging outside the cafe, studied them as they walked their horses toward the saloon, a rickety, two-story building.

Slocum glanced at the horses outside the saloon, and examined the hoofprints, but read nothing useful. He tossed the reins of his roan around the hitching bar, ignoring the stares of two bearded men sitting on the porch rockers.

It was a spacious saloon with three tables for poker, and a long bar with plenty of customers. Some women lounged at the tables. Tad trailed behind Slocum, who headed for the bar. Waiting for the barkeep, Slocum turned to examine the men. They were a rough, ragtag crew: cowboys, drifters, and gamblers. But he did not see a gang of hardcase killers. Red Creek looked like the wrong move. It had been a waste coming here. They should have gone to Aurora. The barkeep, his bald head shiny and perspiring, finally came up.

"Reilly's the name. What's it to be, mister?"

"I'm Slocum, whiskey for me, a beer for the young one."

After Reilly slapped down the drinks, Slocum leaned forward. "Say, Reilly, I'm lookin' for a gang of six men, might have passed through, might even be here."

The barkeep examined Slocum with gray noncommittal eyes.

"We get all sorts, pardner. Got names?"

"No, no names. Just a bunch, six men."

Reilly looked doubtful. "I haven't seen six together."

Slocum emptied his glass, and Reilly refilled it, staring at him curiously. "What'd they do?"

"A mean bunch," Slocum said grimly.

"You a lawman, mebbe?"

"No."

Reilly found the lean, green-eyed hombre interesting. He glanced at Tad, sipping his beer delicately. "Lemme understand, mister. You aim to tackle this mean gang, six of them, you and this young fella?"

Slocum nodded. He surveyed the men at the bar, then those at the playing tables. "Any strangers come in?"

Reilly looked thoughtfully around the saloon. "Danker, that's the laughing hombre at the poker table in the brown hat, thick mustache. He came in hours ago, did some hard drinking, took Inez upstairs, came down, and been playing cards and laughing ever since."

Slocum studied Danker, a burly man with mean, small eyes. He had a pile of winnings and looked pleased. He'd just won another hand, and gloated as he raked in the pot.

He couldn't be much if he gloated over losers. That was
no reason to believe he belonged to the killer gang, but he
was a stranger, and he'd come in at about the right time.
"Get another beer," he told Tad, and strolled to the table
where five players were concentrating on their cards. Of
them all, only Danker glanced up, gave Slocum a piercing
look, then went back to his cards. At the end of the next
pot, an old-timer with a grizzled face pushed back his chair.
"These cards are rotten," he complained.

"Nothing wrong with 'em, pop," grinned Danker, his
white teeth shiny under his bushy mustache.

"If I had your luck, I'd say that, too, Danker," said the
grizzled cowboy.

Danker showed his teeth. "Cards ain't a game of luck.
It's a game of brains."

One of the other players, a cowboy with a big nose
and gray eyes, who had been losing, glowered. "Game o'
brains? So how come you're winning?"

Danker froze and studied the speaker. "Jones, I should
put a bullet up your ass for that, but I got a lot of your
money, and figger you got a right to be riled. So I'm givin'
you that remark. Don't make another."

Jones flushed. He didn't know Danker from a hole in
the wall. Danker had walked into the saloon, guzzled at
the bar, screwed Inez, then come into the game and started
winning. What burned Jones was that *he'd* been winning
until Danker turned up. By making room for Danker in the
game, that polecat had landed in his seat; therefore Danker
had been getting *his* cards. That left a bad taste. The trouble
was, Jones didn't know how good Danker was with a gun.
He talked mean, and you didn't talk like that unless you
were a fool or pulled a fast gun. Jones looked up at the

lean, green-eyed hombre standing over the game, studying Danker like he didn't think much of him. Well, who would, a man who gloated when he beat your hand?

Jones lit a cigar. After all, he was no slouch himself when it came to the fast draw; he'd done his share of shooting and was still around. But there was no point in pushing Danker into a draw, since he'd been the one to make the remark about brains. Still, it rankled that all this time Danker had been pulling *his* winning cards.

When the old-timer stood up, Slocum spoke softly. "Reckon I'll get in, if nobody's got objections."

The men shrugged. Danker glanced at Slocum as if he were a bug.

"We don't care who's playin', long as you got money to lose."

"Don't aim to lose," Slocum replied.

Danker grinned. "Nobody aims to lose, but it happens." He glanced at his winnings. He liked money, but even more, he liked to beat his opponents.

They started to play again and the next few pots were small. Then Slocum found himself betting against Danker and Jones, the others having dropped out. He had two pair, queens high, and figured it was worth a good pot. But he was more interested in the gunman in front of him, who looked like he had a history of crimes behind him.

"Just hit town, Danker?" he asked.

Danker looked up from under his low brown hat, his black eyes intense and steady as he measured Slocum. He grinned slowly. "Sure. And I'm hitting this game like Sherman hit Georgia."

Slocum stiffened. Danker was a bluebelly, and the way he said that, maybe he'd been one of the raiding, rampaging dogs who put Georgia to fire and sword. Slocum put a rope on his feelings; he could be wrong about him.

"Reckon you rode with Tecumseh Sherman," he said.

Danker's grin widened. "Reckon so, rebel. Hate to fight with a losin' bunch." He glanced at his cards. "I can tell by your accent you're a southern hero."

Slocum studied Danker with cool eyes. Danker was a real charm boy, and he had to think himself a top gun to act like this. But there was no point in fighting, not when he wanted information. "You got a nice way of talkin'," he said quietly.

Then Slocum's mind took an odd turn, thinking about the war. He remembered the carpetbagger judge who, after the war, put a claim on the Slocum plantation, land that had belonged to his ancestors for generations. He remembered the fury as he faced that judge. Yes, he gave that carpetbagger the land, which he could rightly claim forever— six feet deep of it. That's what sent him on the run to the territories, where he'd been drifting ever since.

"You playin' or dreamin', mister?" It was Danker's voice growling.

Slocum stared; he sure looked like the kind of rotten polecat who'd be in on the Five Spots killing. Slocum glanced at the bar where Tad was watching and listening. "No hurry, Danker," he drawled. "You can keep your money a bit longer. I was just wondering if you happened to ride in from Five Spots."

Danker's dark eyes were blank. "You playing a game of twenty questions, mister?"

"I ain't heard your answer," Slocum said.

"Mebbe I did, mebbe I didn't. What the hell difference is it goin' to make?"

Everyone at the table and nearby became silent, aware of the tension between the green-eyed cowboy and the burly gunman.

Slocum tapped the edge of his cards on the table. "Hey, Danker, tell me. Did you know Bill Selby of Five Spots?"

Danker gave Slocum a measured look, the black eyes gleaming dangerously. "Mebbe I did, and mebbe I didn't."

Slocum's voice iced over. "Mister, I'm asking for a straight answer. Did you or didn't you know Bill Selby?"

Danker made a decision. "Yeah, sure. I knew him."

"*Knew* him? Reckon you know he's dead?"

Danker grinned slowly. "They keep dyin', Slocum. Jest between us, you, too, sound like a man headed for a short life."

"You never know, Danker. So where's your sidekicks? I figure there's five more like you."

Danker laughed softly, a man with a lot of confidence. "Yep, you're right. Real smart. We're the Brome bunch, six of us. They rode west to Aurora. Now you know. Who the hell are you?"

Slocum's face was grim. "Brome bunch. Who is Brome?"

"That's the mystery."

"How come you didn't ride with them, Danker?"

"Personal business."

Danker pushed his chair back slowly. "And now, mister, you jest used up all your questions." He showed his teeth in a vicious grin. "Know why I been telling you all this, mister? 'Cause it don't matter. You'll be dead in less than a minute."

The chairs scraped as the men at the table rushed to the walls.

Danker stood up, but Slocum kept sitting. "Would you

mind telling me *why* you all shot Selby?"

"Jest stand up, mister, or I'll hit you where you are," Danker snarled, already in the gunfighter's crouch.

"Hey, you, Danker!" The shrill voice cut through the silent saloon like a knife.

Danker reacted sharply, moving backward so that he could keep Slocum in view, then looked to the bar.

Tad had come forward, a wiry young gunman, his face pale and strained, blue eyes blazing, his hands at his sides. "You shot my father. You're a yellow, rotten bastard."

Slocum felt his flesh crawl, aware of more fear than if his own life was on the line. He watched Danker's hand snake to his gun, as he went for his own gun. Three shots fired. Two bullets crashed into Danker—one to his chest, the other hitting him in the forehead. He toppled back like a sawed tree, a corpse before he reached the floor. His own bullet had gone into the ceiling.

Slocum and Tad stood over him; the blood gurgled up from his chest to stain his shirt and there was a neat hole in his forehead. His black eyes, that just minutes ago shone with scorn, were now empty, and his mustached, arrogant face looked amazingly peaceful.

"They look easy at the end," Slocum muttered. He turned to Tad, stern. "Don't ever do that again."

Tad's face was grim. "He shot my people, Slocum."

Slocum nodded, and his voice softened. "I understand."

Revenge could ease the pain, but they were no closer to understanding the massacre than before. But at least they knew *who* did it. "Did you know this Brome?"

"Never heard of him," Tad said.

3

Next morning, as they rode silently, the sun, a yellow, dazzling ball, climbed the horizon. To their right, the vast, sawtoothed mountains shouldered west. An eagle, surveying the land below, soared south with majestic nonchalance. And once, two deer drinking at a small stream stopped to stare at them, then abruptly turned and scampered for cover.

As he rode, Slocum couldn't help but smile, thinking about Tad—a ballsy kid—how he had insulted Danker, challenging him to draw. Danker was a gunfighter who'd done his killings. And for a split second, Slocum feared for Tad, but that had been unjustified, because the kid was blue lightning.

Slocum, from the start of their mission of revenge, aimed to keep a sharp, protective eye on Tad. There were vicious polecats in the territory. But Selby had given his son the training he needed for self-defense. It took a load off Slocum's mind. He wouldn't have to baby-sit this yearling.

When they stopped to let the horses drink, Slocum said, "Back there in the saloon, boy, you were real fast."

Tad looked pleased. "Dad had me practicin' speed, jerking the gun and shootin' at cans. I did it a lot. He told me I was fast."

Slocum smiled. "Nothing wrong with that. But maybe you stepped in *too* fast."

Tad's eyes narrowed. "Don't see that, Slocum. Danker was in the gang. That's enough for me."

"He's just one. There were six. The Brome bunch. Who are they?"

Tad shrugged. "Don't know, but there's five now."

Slocum ran his hand over the sleek body of the roan. "Maybe we coulda learned *why* they hit your family. Danker was talkin', figurin' himself the best gun. When a man thinks that, he'll tell you anything. He reckons you're dead, and it won't matter what you know."

"S'pose you're right, Slocum. All I could think of was my dad and Seth lying in their blood, and this rotten dog was one of them who did it." He bit his lip.

Slocum could understand Tad's feelings; he had wanted blood for blood as he faced Danker. But the mystery was *why* they did it. Was it the money? How'd they know about it? Maybe it was something else.

They continued on the trail toward Aurora.

They rode west for an hour under a hot, baking sun. Slocum felt sweat under his collar.

Then they smelled the burning.

Tad was staring up the slope and frowning. "That's coming from MacKay's place."

"MacKay? Who's that?"

"Dad's friends. Belle and Charlie MacKay."

Now what? wondered Slocum.

They pushed their horses until they came in sight of the house; it was gutted, but not as badly burned as the Selby ranch. Inside, the rooms were ransacked, furniture kicked around. A lot of searching. For money? There was blood on the floor. Slocum studied the signs. It had the mark of the Brome bunch. Behind the house, someone had been thrown in a shallow grave, the stones piled on.

"It's Charlie MacKay," Tad said, after they picked off some stones.

Slocum lit a cigarillo. "Did a lot of searching, for money. After they killed him, they took his woman, dragged her to a horse."

His green eyes had a cold glitter as he looked west at the looming mountains. "Your dad good friends with the MacKays, Tad?"

"Good friends." Tad looked pale. "And Belle is something. Plenty of woman. I been secretly in love with her."

Slocum looked at the prints. "Brome's got her now. He's got the money, he's killed two men who know each other. I got a feeling that Brome's got something bad sticking in his gut."

Tad thought of his dad, and of Belle. He looked at the grave, the stones piled carelessly over the face of the dead man. He spoke slowly. "When Comanches want to punish a man they tie him, lay him out in the sun, cut his eyelids, cover him with honey for the red ants. That's the kind of killin' I'd like to give Brome."

Slocum sighed. You could scarcely blame the kid for his bloodthirsty sentiments. Slocum tried to sense the kind of man Brome was: He always surprised his victims, he burned, he robbed, and he killed. He didn't take chances.

He had to be clever. Now he had a woman with him. That could be his weak point.

He walked toward their horses. "We better ride fast."

4

Brome's spurs jingled as he got up from the campfire and looked toward the woman sitting alone on a flat rock. The men of his bunch looked at each other, then went on eating.

Brome glanced at two buzzards flying south, at the distant mountains against the light blue sky. He loosened his red bandanna and walked toward the woman. Brome was a powerfully built man with broad cheekbones, gray eyes like pitted stones set wide in a heavy-jawed face. He came close to the woman. She ignored him.

"Reckon you were surprised, Belle," he said.

She said nothing.

"I'm talkin' to you."

She turned slowly and stared at him with luminous blue eyes; they were steady, without fear. "Surprised? Yes, I thought you were dead," she said.

His face hardened. "Brome doesn't die easy."

"As long as he dies," Belle retorted.

Brome's mouth twisted as he stared at her. She had silky honey-colored hair that fell softly around her face, satiny skin, and full, well-shaped lips. Her body was curvy, a slender waist, full breasts, and sensual hips.

Brome lit a cigarillo and remembered that when he was in that hellhole, he had thought about Belle a lot, for a long time, and how he'd get to her.

"But it wasn't me that died," he said. "It was Charlie MacKay."

"You will, too."

He smiled grimly. "Funny thing, Belle, how things go round. If you jest keep waiting."

Her eyes slitted. "I can't wait for you to get the rope."

He laughed. "But who's left to do it, Belle? MacKay is gone."

"Someone will, if there's a God in heaven."

Brome shrugged and looked back at the campfire, where his men were eating and drinking. His bunch, spawned in hell. He could see them from here in the dancing light of the flames: curly, clever Dom, a fast gun; tough, husky Gere Donley, who joked while he killed; Lester, a funny, deadly knife-thrower; and brawny Doc Edwards, with his smart left-handed gun. His hellhole bunch. But where the devil was Danker?

Brome turned back to Belle. She looked like she was smouldering with hate. He liked that. "Ain't nuthin' goin' to help you, Belle," he drawled. "You see, I took care of Selby, too." His eyes glittered at the memory.

Belle's lips tightened. So Bill Selby was gone, too. Her heart wrenched. She had cared for him, too. And his boys, Tad and Seth; she feared for them. She looked toward the campfire, at the men, at Brome. She was alone, then, and they had her. She'd rather be dead; and maybe she'd arrange it. If only she could take Brome with her. The way he had killed Charlie; she tried not to think of it. They had forced her to watch—Brome was like that. Brome had a long memory; he didn't forget anything. He had soaked in poison for two years. And he had come back to kill. Now he had hold of her, and all she could think of was to kill him or kill herself—if she could get a gun, somehow.

Watching her, Brome smiled. "You've got bad thoughts, Belle. But I don't blame you. There's no hurry. I've got some things to do first."

He sauntered to the fire and sat down alongside his men. They looked at him. "We'll go to Aurora tomorrow," he said.

Gere Donley tapped his cigar to drop the ash.

Brome looked at him. "Yeah, what is it?"

Gere grimaced. It always astonished him how Brome could pick up feelings. "It's that woman. I know you feel strong 'bout her, Brome, but I figure it a mistake pickin' her up before we go to Aurora."

"Why's it a mistake?"

"We'll have to leave a man with her, Brome. We might need that man to help on the bank job. Because it looks like Danker ain't making it back."

"I didn't figger Danker would drop out. But it won't matter. Four can do it. In fact, it's better. The bigger the bunch, the more attention you get. I've done plenty of jobs with four men. It's not how many men you have, but how good they are. That's what counts. You, Dom, and Lester will go in with me. Doc will stick with Belle."

Lester rubbed his smooth cheeks. He had a round face,

and almost innocent dark eyes. You'd never think he'd throw a deadly knife. "I hate to say this, Brome, but I don't know *why* we need to hit the bank. We picked up nice swag from Selby and MacKay. We've got plenty of money."

Brome looked at him a long time. "That money, Lester, most of it, is *mine*. I just got it back. Figger it that way. Figger that Selby and MacKay were just holdin' *my* money till I got ready to collect. Now we're goin' to get money for you boys from the bank. Any argument with that?"

Lester's face flushed. "I can see what you mean. But you gotta figger we stuck our necks out, we helped you get that money."

Brome's heavy jaw firmed. "And I'm goin' to help *you* get the bank money. How's that different?"

Lester looked puzzled.

Brome's teeth showed. "Don't bother your head about it. If you don't want to do the bank job, say it."

Lester stared into Brome's gray, deep pitted eyes. "If it means that much to you, we'll do the bank."

Brome nodded. "We're friends again."

He looked at the darkened sky. "Danker went to Red Creek to pay off an old debt. Maybe he paid too much. 'Cause he ain't back. So either that or somebody blasted him in a poker game. We'll forget him."

The men watched Brome walk toward the horses. Gere, a grim smile on his lips, looked at Dom. "What are you thinkin' of?"

Dom smiled. "Of Durante, that's who I was thinkin' of."

Gere said, "That's funny. I was, too."

Brome went to the saddlebag, got out his whiskey bottle, and took a long pull. He looked at the curved line of rocks where they had camped for the night. He took another pull on the whiskey bottle, then he lay back on his bedroll, staring up at the big, silver stars; he remembered Yuma, and seeing the stars, night after night, through the iron bars of his cell while he thought about Selby and MacKay and Belle. He probably had thought about them almost every night that he lay in that hellish cell. Brome hated prison like death; he liked to ride the open country; he liked women, drinking, whiskey, gambling, and to be free. Prison was hell, and his spirit died a little at a time as the days spun by.

He'd lie on the wooden cot in his cell, hands behind his head, imagining how to pay Selby off. The law had grabbed him, and locked him up for years and years. And Selby was the reason. Yes, Yuma was a living death and only the thought of revenge helped him survive.

He began to plan his future; he gathered fellow prisoners, Gere Donley, Jester Lester, Danker, Dom Craig, and Doc Edwards, all hard cases, with their share of kills.

He told them about the Abilene bank job, how he, Selby, and MacKay, working as a team, had robbed the Abilene bank. Did it real smart, without a killing, and went on the run. They got clear up in the Red Hills, in the hut where Belle had been waiting. She'd been with them from the beginning.

They had more money than they'd ever dreamed of, and they celebrated, drinking and drinking. They were drunk when the fracas started about how to split the money. Brome wanted the lion's share for leading the bunch. Selby felt it should be share and share alike.

Belle had cottoned up to Selby, and she backed him. That triggered Brome's jealousy and started the violence. Brome beat Selby to the ground, but didn't finish him off. That had been his mistake. When Brome reached for Belle, she turned away; she couldn't feel right, with all that blood.

He'd drunk so much that he passed out, and later, when he opened his eyes, they were gone, Selby, MacKay, and Belle. The money, too, was gone. He lay in a stupor, thinking about getting up and trailing them. That was when he realized that someone was there, in the hut: the sheriff and four deputies. They chained him and brought him back to Abilene. The banker testified at the trial, and the judge gave him fifteen years at Yuma.

In his second year, Yuma began to crush his spirit. And that's when Durante came into his life.

If it hadn't been for Durante, he'd still be rotting in Yuma, hitting big rocks with a hammer to make them little, under a scorching sun. Oh, Brome didn't mind beating stones, because if he didn't, he'd probably beat his head against the stone walls of his cell to tamp down his rage at Selby.

Durante was a tough prison guard who, whenever they'd meet, would stare coldly into Brome's eyes, then smile wolfishly. Durante was a smart, muscular hombre, who seemed to want to be friendly, and Brome knew why. Durante had looked into the records and learned that Brome had made a big haul out of the Abilene bank, and that the money had never been recovered.

Brome knew Durante was sniffing. He had greed in his heart, and sooner or later, he would talk. It happened three weeks ago, while he was resting against a big rock slab, hidden from the view of the other prisoners. Durante came to sit opposite, where no one could see. He shifted the pistol in his holster, lit a cigar, then said, "Hey, Brome, I always meant to ask you, where'd the money go?"

Brome looked into the man's brown eyes. They were crafty and small. "What money?"

"The money from Abilene, that you stole."

Brome's jaw hardened; he thought about it, about Selby and MacKay, and his feelings jangled so hard he couldn't talk.

Durante looked at him and laughed. "Heard you looted that bank for twenty thousand." He blew smoke toward Brome. "Funny thing, when they found you, you didn't have a lousy buck."

Brome kept silent.

"So the mystery is, where the hell did all that money go?"

"Durante, I figure you a smart hombre. You got a reason for asking that question."

Durante glanced at the prisoners, hard at work. "Brome, I think it's a rotten shame that you're locked away here for years and years, and all that money is rottin' where you probably buried it."

Brome digested that, and smiled grimly. "It is a shame, ain't it?"

Durante just smoked his cigar and waited.

Brome scratched his head: He's telling me he wants a piece of the money, and wants a deal. "Wouldn't it be nice," he said, "if we got together with that money?"

Durante tipped the ash off his cigar. "I'm sure I heard you say we."

"Yup, I said it. We."

"Wonder what you could be thinkin' of?" Durante smiled his wolfish smile.

"You know what I'm thinkin', Durante. Get me outta here, and I'll see that you get a fat piece of that money."

"How fat?"

"Five thousand."

"Ten thousand sounds better."

"That's a lot."

"It leaves you ten, which is a lot better than bustin' rocks here, and watching your life go down the drain."

Brome looked at Durante's broad face, at his muscular arms, at the gun in his holster. "Don't worry about the money. You won't be unhappy."

"How much, Brome? Put it on the line."

Brome thought about it. "Okay, I got a proposition. I know where the money is. And you'll get what you want. But we take five men with us."

Durante's eyes narrowed. "Who you got in mind?"

"Danker, Doc Edwards, Gere Donley, Jester Lester, and Dom Craig."

Durante's eyebrows lifted. "Why do you want 'em?"

"They're good guns, and that's what I need outside."

"Maybe." Durante stroked his chin and coldly studied Brome, staring into his eyes when he said, "How do I know, after you get out, you won't forget the whole thing?"

Brome smiled slowly. "You don't. I can only give you my word."

Durante stood up. "I'll think about it."

A week dragged by, then another, but Durante never said a word, didn't look at him, and Brome felt his spirits sinking. The thought of escape had lifted his spirits sky-high, and he'd begun to think viciously about Selby. But something had cooled Durante down; the breakout seemed to be off. Finally, he found a chance to talk to Durante.

"What's happening?"

Durante stared at him coldly. "You had two partners in that bank job. What about them?"

Brome gritted his teeth. "They got the money. And I'm goin' to pick it off their bones."

Durante looked grim. "I was waitin' for you to get honest with me, Brome."

"I'da tole you, Durante, once we got out. Jest didn't want anything to stop it. But it's goin' to be easy. I know where they are."

Durante studied him with sharp, probing eyes. "I believe you, Brome. All the way. I hate the kind of life I got here. Been lookin' for someone like you. We'll do it. On Sunday, when I take the duty. I'll have the horses ready. Seven of us."

He smiled sardonically. "We'll be the Brome bunch. Tell your men. I know them, they're tough hombres."

They made the break just before sundown, ran for half a mile toward the thickets. Durante had done his job well, greased the right palms, but some dumb guard let the dogs loose, so they were forced to shoot the dogs. After that, there was no serious pursuit. The horses were waiting for them in the thickets.

They started the long trek, hunting what they needed for food and raiding homesteads for clothes and money.

On the night before they got to Five Spots, they sat around the fire drinking whiskey.

Brome thought about Selby and MacKay, yellow-bellied squealers, who had grabbed his loot and beat him of his fair share after the big bank heist. Then he thought about Belle, and licked his lips.

He interrupted his reverie to thoughtfully examine his men as they sat around the fire.

"I'm goin' to the Selby ranch," he told them. "He's got money of mine. Plenty. I'm goin' to collect it. Too yellow to finish me off after he stole my share of the money. I figger he called the law. And that's how I got to Yuma. So, I'm goin' there to teach him."

"Teach him what?" asked Gere with a grin.

"Teach him it's bloody hell to take money from Brome."

"You want us to help?" asked Durante.

"You can watch. But don't think that I'll need you. Still, it's best that we stick together. All for one." He looked at them.

They smiled at each other, and Durante and Danker took out their Colts and spun the barrels.

The next day, at sundown, Brome and his bunch hit the Selby ranch. Gere had been posted on a hill overlooking the spread for the last two hours, watching through field glasses. Brome and the others walked up the hill to join him. They had left their horses picketed back in the grass.

Brome looked at the flaming orange sky. It was a good time of day to do some dirty work. He turned back to Gere.

"There's just Selby and a kid down there, that's it," Gere said.

Brome frowned. "One kid? What about the woman?"

"No woman. He doesn't seem to do much, just sweats his hosses."

"What's he doin' now?"

"Gone in the house for eats with the kid."

Brome looked through the field glasses. It was a nice spread: a well-built house, a spacious corral, fine looking horses. He was living off the bank money, Brome thought.

He wondered about Belle. Where the hell would she be? With MacKay? She liked him, too. Maybe she didn't go for the idea of caring for Selby's kids. He had two. Where was the other? Dead, maybe? Kids died easily in the territories. What did it matter? Again Brome thought of Selby and he could taste the bile.

He'd catch Selby at dinner. Always a good time, Brome figured, to hit a man while he was eating; his guard tended to be down, he was lulled by food and drink.

"Let's go," he said. "Durante and Danker with me inside, Gere and Lester outside. Move soft. Doc and Dom, you go back to the horses and wait. When you hear gunfire, bring them on down to the ranch house."

Selby had finished his supper and was sipping coffee, studying his son, Seth, at the other end of the table. Selby thought of Seth's mother, Abigail; the boy had her eyes, blond hair, and smiling ways. Selby felt sadly nostalgic, remembering her, how she'd died, giving birth to Seth. He felt a pang. It seemed unfair, trading a life for a life; a mystery.

Selby could have used a mother for Tad and Seth, and he'd hoped Belle would step in. But Belle didn't like the idea of a ready-made family. Selby understood. She was entitled to start her own, and who could blame her? When she went with MacKay it had been a jolt because Selby really cared for Belle. But he knew you didn't get everything you wanted.

Seth had finished eating and was taking the dishes to the kitchen. A good kid, five years old, always smiling.

Selby poured more coffee and raised his cup. He suddenly thought of Brome. He, too, had been crazy about Belle.

It was why, that fateful night after they hit the bank, that Brome and he had that bloody, knockdown fistfight. Selby believed there was always trouble if you took a woman into the game. After that fight they broke away from Brome. Selby had come to the town of Five Spots, where he bought this spread with some of the bank money. Belle lived with MacKay. You had to take such things in stride.

Funny things happened in a man's life, Selby thought. He had a recent letter from John Slocum, his wartime sidekick, saying he expected to pass through Five Spots in the next weeks. Selby felt it'd be nice going over old times with Slocum. It had been a rotten war; they'd suffered from everything: hunger, hurt, and the death of fighting mates.

Selby's face tightened. It was after the war that things really got bad for him. He had a wife and a kid, and lousy prospects. He hated it, he'd fought for the cause, and after the war, it was hell, too. The carpetbaggers and the scavengers were picking the bones of the Confederacy. Then his wife had died giving birth to Seth. It had been a bad time. It was not too long after that when he met Brome and MacKay. They talked about it: They'd make one strike, hit a bank. What did they have to lose? And a win could mean big money. They could all start a new life.

And that's what happened. They did the bank job, smart and easy. Everything went like clockwork; nobody was shot, and they got away clear. Twenty thousand dollars. But Brome was a coldhearted bastard, which Selby didn't discover till later. The bad stuff started *after* the bank job, in that hideaway hut where they met with Belle.

Selby sighed, sipped his coffee. Dinner had been quiet because Tad, his older son, was visiting his pal at the

Davis ranch. And Seth, his smiling, blond five-year-old, was playing in the kitchen.

Then Selby picked up the sound. His hand went to his gun, but a voice growled from the window behind him, "Don't move, mister."

There was more than one intruder. Selby could hear them. Who the hell were they? Drifters? He lived modestly. Nobody knew he had money. They had the draw; he'd go with it.

The voice growled, "Pull your gun slowly and drop it."

He dropped the gun on the floor.

Then the front door opened and Selby stared. A queer feeling shot through him. He didn't like the look in those pitted gray eyes.

"Brome, is it you?"

"How's it goin', Selby?" Brome smiled, like a jackal. He could scarcely believe it. In jail, over and over, he had dreamed this, and now it was true.

Seth came in, curious, smiling, looking at his father. Selby's face was tight. "Whyn't you go out and play, Seth."

"Don't go too far, Seth," Brome said.

Seth frowned, then smiled because he always found grown-ups were fun, even this strange cowboy with the mean eyes. He went out the door. He passed two tough-looking hombres who came through the door, guns in hand.

Brome smiled. "My boys." He looked around. "You've got a nice place, Selby. But I expected you'd be livin' better."

"Why so?"

"Well, you got plenty o' money."

Selby said nothing.

"What about Belle? Thought she'd be here."

"She's with MacKay." Selby was puzzled. From his voice, you couldn't tell if Brome had hard feelings, but two tough hombres were holding their guns on him.

"Surprised to see me, Selby?"

"Well, I didn't think your time was up."

"It's not *my* time that's up." Brome smiled again, wolfishly.

Selby's jaw hardened. He didn't like any of this.

"But to answer your question, Selby, my time wasn't up. I got sprung. My good friend, Durante." He poked his thumb at the burly, rugged man on the right with the Colt. The man's eyes were blank, telling nothing—a poker player.

"Yes, Durante came along and said, 'Hey, Brome, what's a rich fella like you doin' in jail? Gimme some money and I'll get you out.'" Brome stopped and waited.

"Well," said Selby, "you got plenty of money. Your share."

Brome's eyes glowed dangerously.

Selby looked puzzled. "Are you blamin' me?"

"For what?"

"For gettin' caught, for jail?"

Brome slowly nodded. "I'm blamin' you. I know a double-crossin' yellow dog when I see one."

Selby looked at him and thought desperate thoughts. "You came here because you thought I double-crossed you and squealed to the law?"

Brome nodded and grinned. "You got it now; you and your sidekick, MacKay. And Belle."

There was a long silence.

When Selby spoke, his voice was harsh. "You got it wrong, Brome. After that fight, I was hurt bad. I didn't want any part of you. I took my share, *just my share*. And I left."

Brome's jaw was hard. "You're a liar. Too yellow to tell it straight. You got beat, you hated my guts, you and MacKay took Belle and all the money, and you told the law where to find me."

Selby shook his head. "You're not seeing it."

"Oh, I'm seein' you livin' out here, sweet and easy, while I been breakin' my back, breakin' rocks. That's what I been seein'." He pulled his gun. "Hog-tie him." Gere and Dom prepared to tie Selby's arms and legs. Selby watched Brome. His own gun was still on the floor. "Now," Brome said, "where's the money?"

A silence. "I told you—we left your share."

"Bring the kid," Brome said.

Durante brought Seth in. The boy looked puzzled.

"A nice looking kid, ain't he?" Brome signaled Durante, who put his gun against the boy's head.

"Now," said Brome, "where's the money?"

Selby quivered. "Are you crazy?"

"The money?"

"It's in the strongbox, buried in the flooring behind the bed."

Brome looked at Gere. "Go and look."

They stood there, Durante holding the kid with the gun at his head, Brome and the others with guns on Selby.

Gere dragged the locked strongbox into the living room. Brome shot it open and looked in. "Where's the rest?"

"That's it. I tole you, I took my share."

Brome's eyes glared. "You got ten seconds."

Selby's body shook. He wanted to hurl himself on this madman, destroy them all. "It's the truth," he said.

Brome turned to Durante. "Shoot the kid, Durante."

"Don't—please." Selby's voice was agonized.

Durante cleared his throat.

"I gave you an order," Brome said.

Durante scowled. "I didn't sign on to shoot kids," he said.

Brome's move was lightning fast; he shot Durante right between the eyes. Selby crawled for his gun. Brome wheeled and shot Selby in the shoulder. Selby tried to keep going, but another bullet in the gut stopped him.

Brome leaned down, his voice quiet. "The rest of the money—where is it? You got one second." Selby was all torn up, but his gun on the floor was within his reach. He looked at it. Seth, in fear, started to run to the door.

Brome turned quickly and shot the boy, who fell without a sound.

Selby screamed in agony, and with a superhuman effort, flung himself at the gun, brought it up to fire, just as three guns blasted him. Brome kept firing. It took eight bullets to kill Selby.

Brome looked at his shoulder. It was bleeding.

He turned to the others. "MacKay's got the money," he said, looking down at the bloody floor. "We'll get it there." He turned to the men watching him. "Durante's dead. You men will get his share. Burn the damn house."

Brome went out into the night. It was dark now, the moon a big silver ball, and he thought how nice it looked behind the jagged bulk of the mountains.

Slocum glanced at the sky. It was overcast, with white strung-out clouds, the threat of a quick squall. They had been riding toward Aurora for some time, with Tad moody, Slocum silent and thinking. The Brome bunch, two days ago, had headed for Aurora. They had money and, Slocum figured, they'd try to spend some of it: drinks, women, and supplies. Would men like these stay in a town like Aurora? No, they'd move on and, if he guessed right, they'd leave a path of crimes behind.

Slocum thought about Brome, wondered who he was, and what made him kill so viciously. Slocum had counted eight wounds in Selby's body. There had to be terrible rage behind that kind of shooting. And what about the bullet in the kid! Slocum felt a scalding anger. It was the act of a crazy killer. Such men didn't deserve to walk God's earth.

He glanced at Tad, riding the gelding alongside. A good-looking youngster with a strong, square face and a hurt look deep in his clear blue eyes, a look that wouldn't leave until blood paid for blood.

They had been climbing a rise strewn with bushes and shrubs when they heard a single shot and a cry. It came from the trail to their left, on the other side of the rise.

Slocum glanced at Tad. "Let's have a look."

Tad scowled. "Let's stick to our business, Slocum."

Slocum's eyes narrowed. "This may be our business. Hostile Comanches, outlaws, thieves. Best to know."

Tad looked thoughtful, but didn't like it. "We could bog down with it, Slocum. I'm after Brome."

"It's good to know who's shooting in your neighborhood." Slocum began to ride forward, and after a moment, Tad followed.

Then they heard the pounding hooves, and saw the two strong bays pulling a wagon come into sight at their left. A man lay sprawled on the wagon seat. He'd been shot, and to

Slocum, he looked gone. A young woman in a blue dress, cracking the whip, kept urging the horses, and the wagon bounced and jostled over the stony, uneven ground.

As Slocum moved forward he saw two riders in pursuit, guns in hand. Grimy, sleazy-looking men, clearly drifters. Maybe they had happened on the couple in the wagon and hoped to make a killing.

When the drifters saw Slocum and young Tad, it set doubts in their minds. They had already killed the rider, and their intentions with the woman were obvious. Now, they would either have to run for it or settle with the newcomers. They started shooting at Slocum and Tad.

Slocum felt two bullets whistle past him. He heard Tad cry out, obviously hit. Slocum's gun spit three times and the men jerked crazily on their horses and dropped.

The woman saw what happened, pulled on the reins, bringing the wagon to a stop. She watched Slocum turn to his young companion, who was holding his shoulder. Then she bent to examine the man lying beside her on the seat.

Slocum rode to the men sprawled on the ground. They were stone dead: two bearded, mangy men in grimy Levi's, clearly scavengers of the trail. They probably thought they had stumbled on easy prey.

Slocum loped back to Tad, who seemed in pain.

"Let me see." Slocum examined the wound. A bullet was lodged in his left shoulder; it would have to be dug out. Tad looked aggrieved, not that he'd been hit, but that it might hinder his search for Brome and his gang.

The woman in the wagon was staring at the man on the seat when Slocum rode up and dismounted. The man had been hit in the head.

He had a worn, lined face, and looked much older than

the woman. She had dark hair and gray eyes in a lovely, creamy face. "He's dead," her voice was flat.

Slocum nodded. He wondered if the man was her father, but he didn't seem quite old enough. The wagon was loaded with grain, seeds, and supplies. Apparently they'd shopped in Aurora and, on the way back to their home, had run afoul of the two mangy dogs. She looked at the thieves, lying in their blood.

"You killed them." Her eyes glowed. "Thank you. God knows what might have happened if you didn't come along." She glanced at Tad. "And you're wounded. I'm sorry. We live just a few miles south of here. I could help you clean that up."

"We oughta keep goin'," Tad said.

"You've got a bullet in there," Slocum said. "We'll have to pick it out."

"I'd like to keep ridin'."

Slocum's mouth hardened. "Let's take care of your arm first."

Tad looked angry. Slocum turned away, aware of what Tad was thinking. This wouldn't have happened if they'd stuck to the Brome business. Well, you never knew what life had around the next corner; it could be a fist, a bullet, or a woman.

"I'm Mady Gilbert." She pointed to the dead man. "He's George. Was my husband."

That surprised Slocum. He had figured the man was either her older brother, uncle, or even her father.

They drove four miles to her place, a small spread with some cattle, chickens, and a few horses.

Slocum wondered why Mady, a lovely young woman, would marry a man at least twenty years older.

Slocum dug the grave and they buried George. To Slocum's practiced eye, Mady was not exactly overpowered with grief. She poured whiskey over Tad's wound, and Slocum picked the bullet out. Tad grimaced with pain. It would take time, Slocum figured, for Tad to get back to working order. He'd lost plenty of blood.

Mady gave them a good dinner, and afterward, she brought out good whiskey, and they drank a lot, it being a troubling time. She became teary and confidential. She told them she'd been raised by her father, and that George had been a family friend; she'd seen a lot of him when growing up. When her father died, she'd been deeply grieved, and George stepped in with comfort and security, so she married him, a gentle, kind man, and she learned to care, but it had never been love.

"Maybe I don't know what love is," she said, taking another drink. "Love is nice, but maybe it's not necessary. A good, kind man is important, too."

Slocum smiled, and couldn't help looking at her abundant breasts, her full hips. "A woman should get more than just kindness from a man."

"That right?" she said.

They talked, and Mady told them they could stay as long as it took for Tad to heal, longer if they wanted. She could always use a man around the ranch. She took the dishes to the kitchen. They heard her go outside with grain to feed the horses.

Tad looked grim. "We've got a job to do."

"How you goin' to do it? You ride now, you'll bleed to death."

"Damn you, Slocum."

Slocum gazed at him innocently.

"I tole you, we shoulda stuck to our business. But you hadda push your nose out." Tad showed his teeth.

Slocum lit a cigarillo. "If we didn't, those two polecats would have raped Mady, sure as you're settin' there."

Tad squirmed at the thought. "And what about Brome? Is he just gonna ride off free, keep on killin'?"

"I'm goin' after him, now. I'll ride to Aurora. After you fix up, you go there. If I ride off, I'll leave word in the saloon. That okay?"

Tad looked sullen. "I want to be at the showdown with Brome."

"Sure." Slocum stroked his chin. "Meanwhile, you got this fine setup. A good-looking woman, feeling grateful. Remember this; you helped save her from a fate worse than death."

"What the hell's that mean?"

"Ever have a woman, Tad?"

"That's a hell of a question!"

"Well, she's a full-blooded woman, and she's got a lot of hunger. Her husband's gone. He didn't give her much. She's goin' to be mighty lonely, mighty quick. A good time for you to learn about the pleasure a woman can give a man."

Tad let out a breath. "Damn your hide, Slocum, if you aren't one horny polecat."

Slocum smiled and rose to his feet. "If anyone's a horny polecat, it should be a young stallion like you. Now, I'm going after that bunch. I'm not in a terrible hurry to tackle five mean killers by myself. So you just hurry and get strong and come ridin' up to Aurora to help."

He went out the door. It was night and the vast, dark blue sky was sprinkled with a multitude of silver stars. A soft breeze carried the scent of prairie wildflowers.

Mady came from the corral toward him, carrying a pail. She had full, rounded arms, a rounded bosom, and a slender waist.

He couldn't help but smile in the face of such abundant femininity. "Take care of Tad. He's got a lot on his mind. Might need to forget his troubles."

"We all need to forget our troubles." She glanced toward the new grave, then looked back at him.

He sensed a woman who was hungry. Too bad, he thought, that he couldn't stay put. Mady looked like a woman who liked to pleasure a man. He smiled, thinking that she might be just right for bringing Tad to manhood. He walked to the roan and she followed him. She looked deep in his eyes when he turned.

"Thank you, Mr. Slocum, for what you've done." She took his hand and pressed it against her.

In his mind, he cursed his bad luck that he had to go and was passing her to Tad, who might not appreciate it.

He swung his leg over the saddle. Her eyes were glittering. "Good-bye, Mady. We may meet again."

She stood there, a ghostly figure in the night, watching him ride away, until she lost sight of him in the shadows of the crags.

5

When Brome and his bunch reached Aurora, the sun still shone fiercely, pouring heat on the town. Brome walked his sweating horse down the dusty main street, lined with weathered two-story buildings. He looked at Kelly's Livery, Martha's Cafe, at the general store. When they reached the Aurora bank, he tossed a casual glance at it, but his sharp eyes missed few details. There were two guards, one outside, one inside. Lots of money to protect, he thought. The guard in the doorway with two guns eyed the burly strangers riding past with curiosity. Brome's men, however, just stared at the big saloon sign, down the street, showing no interest in the bank.

Several dust-covered cowboys, who had been running cattle up the trail, had come into Aurora, and were drifting around town to buy supplies and relax in the saloon.

Brome liked that; they brought money to town, and the money went from the stores to the bank. Some of that money might end up in the pockets of his bunch.

Brome smiled. No hurry. But he didn't like the way the men had jogged past the bank with nary a look. Not smart. Brome thought of Belle. He'd left her in a trail hut with Doc to keep an eye on her. Doc, a trusted, solid hombre, would handle her nice and easy. Later, he, Brome, would handle her in his own style.

They reached Riley's Saloon, dismounted, and threw their reins on the hitchrack.

"I need whiskey," Gere said, taking his hat off. "My mouth's dry as Death Valley." Brome looked at Gere Donley with his innocent, round blue eyes, high forehead, dark hair; he was funny, but gristle-tough, a hard puncher.

"I'm thirsty, too," said Dom Craig grinning at Brome. "Lots o' sand to wash outta my throat."

"Whiskey and women for what ails us," said Lester, mopping his brow.

They stood there in the shade of the saloon building. Can this bunch crack the bank? Brome wondered. He turned to gaze back down the dusty street. "I think we oughta mosey back and take a careful look."

"Why?" asked Gere.

"You aimin' to rob a bank, you might look at it," Brome said.

Gere scowled. "The bank ain't goin' anywhere. Meanwhile, we got this big thirst."

"Yeah," said Lester. "We been ridin' under a fryin' sun. We've got a thirst."

"We're all thirsty," Brome said, "but business comes first. You boys mosey up there, separately, and take a look at the layout."

"You figger we need to do that?" asked Gere.

"Yeah, I figger that. And look good at what's near the bank. Chances are it's not inside the bank where you catch hell, but after. When you're ridin' hard with the money, and sure you made the getaway and that you're suddenly rich. Then the bullets come outta somewhere and rip your head off. Better look at the layout so you know where you're goin'."

"Robbin' a bank," said Dom, "ain't such a big deal. You point a gun and ask for the money. If they don't deliver, you shoot, then take the money."

Brome's eyes narrowed. "There's more bank robbers in Boot Hill than anywhere else, because they thought like that. Robbin' a bank is like makin' a getaway from the Yuma jailhouse. You gotta know what you're doin'."

They looked at him, then one at a time, they all went back, Gere and Lester on one side of the street, Dom and Brome on the other, drifting cowboys having a look around town. Gere, as he walked, couldn't help thinking of Durante. It had been Durante who plotted the Yuma escape, and Brome owed him ten thousand dollars. Brome shot him; a neat way to wipe off a debt. Gere figured it was something to keep in mind about Brome.

Gere noted the solidly built bank building, the guard with his two guns posted at the door. He glanced at the nearby stores, then started back toward the saloon. They regrouped about thirty feet from the saloon when Gere, his blue eyes staring, said, "Hey, looka there."

A grimy cowboy in beat-up Levi's and a brown, peaked hat, pushed low over his eyes, had come out of the saloon, walked unsteadily to Gere's pinto and swung up in the saddle.

Grim-faced, Gere stepped quickly ahead of the others

and, as the rider came past, he grabbed the reins.

"What the hell you doin'?" growled the rider.

"Where you goin' on my hoss?" asked Gere.

"Your hoss?" The cowboy glared. "Step outta my way, you crazy polecat." He looked drunkenly around at some men at the porch.

Gere's jaw went granite hard, but he controlled himself. "Hey, jughead, mebbe you got a bit too much whiskey. Take a good look and you'll see you're ridin' the wrong hoss."

The drunk cowboy didn't bother to look at the horse; he just seemed to be in a hurry and in a rage. "Reckon I know my own hoss. Turn those reins loose before I fill yuh fulla holes."

Brome scowled. He didn't want a scuffle with this drunk, didn't care for the attention, if it was avoidable. He moved up, smiling, pushed Gere aside and crooked his finger at the cowboy. "Hey, I think you got the right hoss, and this here hombre's a little loco. Lean down, I want to tell you somethin'."

The drunk smiled broadly and bent forward. Brome jerked him off the horse, spun him around and slammed a short right to his chin. He went down like a sack of stones.

The men on the nearby porch laughed.

"Know him?" Gere asked.

"Just a stray with a headful of whiskey," said one old-timer.

"He's lucky, for a horse thief," said Brome, studying the drunk.

He turned and walked toward the saloon, followed by the others. Gere retied his pinto's reins to the hitchrack.

6

Jester Lester, with a smile of pleasure on his face, carried a bottle of whiskey over to the Brome bunch, sitting at a back table.

"That cuts the dust," said Gere tossing off a drink.

"A man needs a bit of fun," said Dom.

Brome drank three whiskies fast, feeling the burn in his throat and gut, then looked around.

It was a spacious, smoky saloon. A square mirror hung behind the bar and dark wood shelves were piled with whiskey bottles; a clock and a picture calendar hung on the wall. About eight cowboys, their faces flushed with drinking, lined the bar. From the other end of the saloon, the sound of money came from poker games.

And, sitting nearby were three women: a blonde, a redhead, and a brunette; they looked lush and buxom.

Dom had been watching the women. "Speakin' o' fun—"

But Brome frowned; one of the hulking, big-boned men

at the bar reminded him of Stryker, who he'd known back in the Yuma prison. Brome wasn't happy about that; he intended to ransack the local bank, and it was smart to know who was around. "I'll be back," he said to his men. He walked to the bar and took a spot next to the big-boned man.

It was Stryker.

This polecat had done his time in Yuma and had been released six months ago. So, what the hell was he doing here, in Aurora? When the barman came up, Brome ordered a whiskey.

Stryker, who had been laughing and talking with two men, turned and spotted Brome. Stryker had shot a man in a meaningless fight. He was not a criminal, just a man who lost his temper. He got only six months in Yuma.

"Brome?" he said, "I don't believe it! How'd you get here?"

"On a horse, Stryker, how the hell did you think?"

Stryker examined him with a cynical grin. "You got out plenty fast. I figure you in Yuma for five more years."

Brome shrugged. "Maybe I got out for being a good boy."

Stryker grinned. "Yeah, and maybe you made a break-out."

Brome picked up his whiskey and drank it. "So, how'd you get to this blasted town?"

"It's my hometown, Aurora. I work here."

"Yeah, at what?"

"I ride shotgun on the Aurora stage." He jerked his finger at the two men alongside. "They're stage men, too."

Brome stared. "That's a helluva job for a graduate of the Yuma Pen."

Stryker grinned. "Well, I didn't go there for thievery,

like you boys." He studied Brome. "So, what are *you* doin'
in Aurora?"

"Jest passin' through."

Stryker's eyes narrowed. "Yeah, let's hope. A bank ain't
safe when you're in town."

Brome's gray eyes glinted. "Oh, I'm through with all
that."

Stryker didn't look convinced. "Try and keep it that way,
Brome. I've got money in that bank. Wouldn't like someone
running off with it."

Brome picked up his drink. "You've got a sense of humor,
Stryker. Try not to use it."

He went back to the table, and could feel Stryker's eyes
on his back.

"Who the hell was that?" said Gere.

"Stryker, one of the boys from Yuma. He left before you
got there."

"I remember him," said Dom. "Not much."

"So what's he doin' here?" asked Lester.

"Riding shotgun for the Aurora stage."

"He'll be trouble," said Dom.

Brome smiled coldly. "Nobody's goin' to be trouble."

"To hell with him. All this talk is distractin'." Gere turned
toward the blonde again, admiring her plump, curvy body.
"Now, look at that blonde. If I had a harem, I'd make her
Number One."

Dom grinned. "Harem? I can see it. You keeping ten
women happy."

Jester Lester smiled. "You think maybe you could satisfy
one woman?"

Brome scowled. "You can't satisfy a saloon girl. Why
try it?" He didn't like whores, but it wasn't easy to get a

decent woman. He thought of Belle and wet his lips. He had some nice ideas about her, once things settled.

Gere looked at the blonde and drooled. "Like Dom says, a man needs a bit o' fun. That blonde."

They turned to Brome. "It's a matter of time," Brome said.

"Do we have time or not?" said Gere.

"Maybe not," said Brome.

The men looked at each other in silence.

"You got Belle," said Gere, "and we got nuthin'. Is that how you want it, Brome?"

Just then the blonde, sticking out her lush breasts, got up and, swiveling her full hips, walked to where a burly, swarthy hombre was drinking and sat down. He showed a great set of white teeth and pushed his bottle at her.

"See that?" said Gere.

"When you're thinkin' of a bank," Brome said, "it's a good idea to concentrate."

"There's time for that," said Gere. "Now I'm concentrating on her."

Brome's gaze fixed on Gere. He's a nervy polecat, he thought, but I need him and the others. "What about the hombre?"

"He'll move."

"And if not? He doesn't look easy."

Gere's hand went lightly over his holster. "I got persuadin' ways."

"Then we get a situation. Seems smart to keep things quiet, not make a stink if you intend to rob a bank." Brome's voice grated.

Gere looked at Dom who, until this time, hadn't said much. "How do you figger it?"

Dom thought, then turned to Brome. "I figger we did our bit for you. We rode a long way, did a lot of blasting. You got money, *your* money, and the woman, Belle. What have we got?"

"Reckon we oughta make time for us," said Gere.

Brome poured another whiskey, and drank it. These boys, he was thinking, had no thanks in them, didn't know what tough times were. He had come out of Tennessee, the backwoods, the shack where his alcoholic father—till he croaked—beat his ass. He'd gone west and, before he was eighteen, he killed his share of men in shoot-outs. He had jerked these jailhouse polecats, now sitting with him, out of Yuma, a living hell. He did it, with Durante. His gun was fastest, he was smartest, and he was the leader. But they didn't care. They had been tough boys who learned wrong ways; they screwed up and landed in Yuma. *He* got them out. Now they were bucking him, his judgment. Well, let them screw their brains out. Maybe it'd go better that way. He might think of something later.

"Okay, go screw your heads off. The bank will close in two hours. If it closes, we'll have to stick in this mangy town another day."

The men smiled at each other.

Gere looked at the blonde and the hombre. They were sitting and talking. He stood, walked to the bar, ordered a whiskey, then turned to stare openly at the blonde. She had a plump, curvy body and shapely breasts. She returned his bold stare with one of her own, and her dark eyes smiled.

The hombre also stared at Gere. "What's the matter?" he asked.

"Maybe it's you," said Gere. "Sitting with her *forever*."

The man smiled. "I'm here as long as I'm here."

Gere looked thoughtfully at the hombre, hulking, broad-shouldered, with black eyes, a thick nose, and drooping mustache. He had a worn holster, a shiny butt on his gun. "Why don't you be nice and go have a lie down somewhere."

The hombre smiled. "Maybe I'll do that later, but for now, why don't you take your pink gringo face out to the livery? There's plenty of horseshit there for you."

Gere grinned back at him. "Step away from the woman. I'm goin' to knock you out the window."

The hombre nodded solemnly. "Let us see who goes out the window." He slowly got to his feet.

"Just a minute." It was Brome, standing eight feet away.

The hombre stared at the powerful gringo with the lean, hard face. "We don't want a rumpus," Brome said. "No bloody fight, no broken jaws and tables. Be a good fellow, and take a walk. That way nobody gets hurt."

The hombre smiled grimly. "Maybe you're the big brother. Maybe you fix everything for him? But who will fix it for you?"

The woman spoke to the hombre. "Pedro, please go quietly. I don't like the sound of guns."

The hombre didn't look at her. "And I don't take orders, 'specially from these. Look at them. They are like buzzards."

Brome stared at the woman and what she saw in his eyes made her stand and walk to the side.

"No," said Gere, glancing hard at Brome. "Let me take this."

"There isn't time."

Brome faced the hombre. "I ask you again: Go quietly." He crouched a bit. "Or pull your gun."

The hombre wet his lips. "You sound like the boss of dying. All right, I go quietly." His smile was twisted. He turned, walked three steps, then stopped and turned.

"No, I change my mind." And his hand darted to his holster.

Brome's move was a streak, the bullet hitting the hombre's chest. He staggered back, went down. He looked at Brome, cursed, and, holding his gun, struggled to bring it up. But he couldn't.

Brome watched him.

Then the hombre died.

Gere bit his lip. "Brome!"

"Don't say anything. Take the woman." Brome's face was stony.

Gunfights were sudden in the saloon and quickly cleaned up. It took little time before the men were again drinking at the bar and playing poker at the tables.

The blonde, however, was waiting at the foot of the stairs. Gere walked to her. She looked at him, then started up the stairs.

Gere followed, his eyes on the level of her buttocks, watching their movement with pleasure. As soon as he shut the door, she pulled her dress over her head, dropping it to the floor. Her breasts were full, her skin silky, her body voluptuous. She had full hips and well-shaped legs. She looked sexy as hell. He peeled off his clothes and went toward her. She didn't waste a moment, but bent down. Her passion seemed to have been fired by what had happened in the saloon, for she went at him with lust, her moves skillful and intense. After a while, she stepped back suddenly, and lay on the bed. He went between her sensuous thighs, deep into her, and began to drive. This was his first woman since prison and he drove like a wild stallion. It didn't take her long to realize she had a man who'd been dreaming women a long time. After it was over, she lay exhausted. Then she started to get up.

Gere turned to her. "Let's do it again."

When he had finally finished, he came down the stairs, and walked to the table.

The men had already been with the other women; they stared at him.

Brome said, "You can't make up for everything you missed in prison."

Gere showed his teeth. "I can try."

Brome looked away, then back at the men around the table. His voice was low. "So now we hit the bank. Listen very carefully." He talked quietly about the bank job.

After a while they went out of the saloon separately. He stayed for a short time and drank.

Twenty minutes later, Brome walked down Main Street. The sun was still warm, though halfway down the sky.

He looked across the street at Lester, standing near the horses, talking to the liveryman. Gere and Dom were on the street, on the far side of the bank.

When Brome put his hand to his hat, Dom, who was watching him, strolled up to the guard at the doorway and said with a broad smile, "Why don't you walk into the bank?"

The husky guard, who had a long face, a heavy drooping mustache, and two guns, scowled. "Are you crazy?"

Dom raised his hand in which a derringer suddenly appeared; he pointed it at the guard's heart. "Maybe, but I don't mind," he said.

The guard gnashed his teeth and turned, as Dom pressed the derringer against his back. In the doorway, still hidden from the bank, Dom said, "Hold it."

The guard paused. He was breathing hard, wondering if he should chance it, grab his two guns. But Dom pulled them from his holsters. "Lotta guns for one man," he said. "Now we wait."

In the bank, Gere came up to the inside guard with a piece of paper. "Mister, can you help me?"

The guard, puzzled, read it: "There's a man at the doorway pointing his gun at you. Take a look."

The guard's eyes glazed for a moment, then turned to see Dom holding a pointed gun hidden in the crook of his arm.

Gere whispered, "Don't move. I'm goin' to take your gun." He reached to the guard's holster and pulled his gun. The guard gritted his teeth.

It was all done so quickly and quietly that only one customer, an old-timer, whose gaze strayed, saw Gere take the guard's gun. His eyes widened.

Gere smiled gently at him and put his finger to his lips.

The old-timer's face crinkled in a grin. He'd seen plenty in his day.

Brome walked to the banker, whose name, Stiller, was carved on a plaque on his big wooden desk. He had a square face and iron gray hair, and was reading something. Against the wall was the steel safe.

Brome sat down in the chair alongside the desk.

Mr. Stiller's piercing eyes looked at Brome, measuring the man, the clothes, the leather satchel at his feet. "Yes, sir, what can I do for you?"

"I'm here to make a big deposit."

Mr. Stiller rubbed his palms. "That's always nice to hear, sir. How much?"

Brome considered. "As much as *you've* got in your bank."

Mr. Stiller worked on that in his mind, and it didn't seem right. "What do you mean, sir?"

"I'm goin' to deposit as much money as you've got in your bank, that's what I mean."

The banker smiled uncertainly. "Like matching?"

"You could call it that." Brome smiled pleasantly.

"That would be a substantial deposit, Mr.—"

"Brome."

Mr. Stiller considered. You never knew about customers. A man could come in looking like this hatchet face with those pitted gray eyes, and still be a hugely successful rancher with thousands of steers. The West was wild, a frontier country, and you couldn't guess who had the money.

"So, what have you got?" Brome asked.

"We've got a balance of close to forty thousand dollars. This is a solid financial institution."

Brome grinned. "That's a good, round number. Well, Mr. Stiller, that's how much I wish to deposit. But I'm afraid I'll have to withdraw it first to deposit it."

The banker scowled, aware that this was a slippery conversation.

"Maybe I missed something, Mr. Brome. I don't understand."

Brome, still smiling pleasantly, leaned forward. "Mister, I'm goin' to withdraw the money from *your* bank and deposit it in *my* bank."

Mr. Stiller's brows knitted.

Brome jerked his finger at the guards.

Stiller looked, saw his guards stripped of their guns, and suddenly understood. He turned pale and groaned. "I pay them good money and when I need them, they're no damned use."

He turned to Brome, his manner hard. "Is your name really Brome? Who the hell are you?"

Brome leaned down and opened the satchel.

"I'm the man who's goin' to make you dead if you don't, quick as hell, get the money out of that safe and into this satchel."

Stiller's pale face looked at the customers, who were now aware of something. Not one there to pull a gun. Sweat broke out on his forehead.

"You can't get away with this, Brome."

"Let's just see. But you don't want to put your life on the line just for the money. Do you?" Brome brought out his gun with amazing speed and put it against the banker's head.

Stiller's eyes popped. He moved to the safe, stooped, and opened it, and looking in, groaned again. *His money*.

"Just breathe easy, you'll get over this," Brome said. "Put it all in the satchel."

Dom and Gere had their guns on the customers while Brome watched Stiller put the money into the satchel. Brome leaned down and closed the satchel.

He stared at Stiller. "Now, the key to the front door."

Stiller, his face pale, reached into his back pocket and pulled out the key.

Brome motioned to Dom, who came over, took the satchel, and walked to the door. Then Brome looked at the few customers, middle-aged and older, who'd been watching it all, fascinated.

"Just stay calm, folks, and nobody gets hurt. Don't try to come outside, or you'll get your head shot off."

Brome and Dom walked to the door where Gere was waiting. Brome looked out. Across the street, Lester lounged, half-hidden in the livery doorway. Their four horses were hitched to the livery post. Down the street, near the cafe, two young cowboys in buckskins were talking.

They went out. Brome locked the door, and they stood on the bank side of the street for a moment.

"Go ahead, Dom, get going," Brome said.

They watched him cross to the horses.

Just then the doors of the saloon swung open and three men, laughing and talking loudly, came out. Brome recognized Stryker, the man he'd known at Yuma, who was now riding shotgun for the Aurora stage. The two men with him, wearing dusty Levi's and guns, worked for the stage, too.

Brome, who'd been holding his gun, slipped it quickly into his holster, as did Gere; they casually started across to the horses.

But Stryker had spotted Brome in front of the bank and seen him holster his gun. He looked at Dom holding the satchel, at Gere, and at the horses. He said something sharply to the men and quickly moved forward.

Gere asked, "Do we run or shoot, Brome?"

Brome's face was hard. "Just walk easy and stay ready."

Stryker came up fast, the two husky men right behind him. "Hold it, Brome. What's in the satchel?"

Brome cursed silently. You plan an easy robbery, but fate steps in and makes a mess. "Meddling is bad business, Stryker. Go back to the saloon."

"Brome, I'm feared it's you who's goin' back—back to Yuma. Tell your boy to drop the satchel."

And so saying, Stryker and the men with him went for their guns. Before they could reach their holsters, three shots, coming from the livery, rang out, and Stryker and the two men crumpled and fell.

Jester Lester, still holding his gun, came out from where he'd been watching, behind the doorway of the livery. Brome and Gere now pulled their guns as they moved to the horses. Dom, with the satchel, swung into his saddle and gave his horse the spurs.

The glass at the bank splintered and someone yelled, "*Bank robbery*. Stop those men!"

Brome cursed as he and Gere swung into their saddles.

The two cowboys at the cafe, startled by the shooting, turned and went for their guns. Brome and Gere fired and the cowboys fell to the ground and lay there.

With Dom riding in front, the four horses sent up a cloud of dust as the Brome bunch galloped west out of town.

Brome cursed, thinking you could plan for everything but the unexpected. In the bank everything had gone right, but it was in the street where chance took over and the shit began to fly. Five men had been shot. A posse would come after them.

In the bank, the teller finally dug up an extra key to open the door and Stiller, his teeth set hard, came out in front of the bank, followed by the two shame-faced guards.

Down the street, Stiller saw the five men sprawled in the dust. "A bloody day." He turned to the brawny guard next to him, looked at his two empty holsters.

"Nice performance, Willard," he said grimly.

Willard swallowed. "That damned polecat jerked a derringer out of his sleeve, Mr. Stiller. Caught me off balance."

Stiller's lip curled. "I'm paying you *not* to get caught off balance, Willard." He looked away; he couldn't afford to be sarcastic, because he, too, got hornswoggled by Brome. A slick bunch.

"Where the hell's Sheriff Cole?"

"He and his deputies rode out to Mill's Point to settle a ruckus in the Dawson family," said Willard.

Stiller put his fingers in his breast pocket, pulled out a cigar, and lit it. "Ride out there. Tell him we got a bigger problem than a family ruckus. The bank is cleaned out of money."

A half hour later Sheriff Cole rode in with Willard and the two deputies, Mac and Todd. Sheriff Cole was a ruddy-faced, big-chested man with a big Stetson and a shiny star. He stopped outside the saloon and said to his deputies, "Go in there and round up a posse."

Then he rode up to the bank. Stiller came out the door, his teeth clamped on a cigar. He wasted no time. "Sheriff, why in hell aren't you around when we need you?"

Cole's jaw hardened. "Mr. Stiller, you're supposed to have a couple of good guns in your bank."

"Good guns. Yeh, but they don't pull 'em at the right time. Those mangy dogs robbed the bank, shot five men. One was Stryker. So get your posse goin' and shoot the hell outta that ornery coyote, Brome." Stiller looked dreamy. "He's one coyote who'd look good in his burial suit. Most of all, sheriff, get that money back or this is goin' to be one piss-poor town."

"Brome, is it?" said the sheriff. "Well, Stryker was a

friend of mine. I aim to pay Brome off with a couple bullets in his damn hide." He turned to look down the street where seven men had spilled out of the saloon and were mounting their horses.

"Don't worry, Mr. Stiller, we'll get that money."

He went to his horse, then turned to the posse trotting up, with Mac in front. When they reached him, he said, "Well, men, let's go shoot some bank robbers."

They set up a holler, started after him, and the clatter of horse hooves sent a huge whirl of dust all the way up Main Street.

7

Slocum rode down Main Street, wide and dusty, and surprisingly quiet, like nothing much was happening. The two-story houses baked in the summer sun, some old-timers loafed on the porches, a couple of women shopped at the general store. From the livery, he could hear the ringing of a hammer on the anvil.

Slocum's jaw tightened as he thought of Brome. Would he still be in town? Why had he come here? He had plenty of money; he'd cracked Selby's strongbox. But you never knew the mind of a killer like Brome. Slocum had met his share of killers, and what they had in common was contempt for human life. In the East, if you didn't like someone, you hit him with your fists; but out here, you hit him with a bullet. This was the frontier, and the one thing that counted was your gun, if you were quick. If you were slow, you were a candidate for Boot Hill.

He rode to Riley's Saloon, and went in. It didn't seem

busy; a few drinkers at the bar, four men playing poker quietly.

Slocum ordered whiskey from Riley, a portly man, with a rugged face and shrewd blue eyes.

"Town looks half asleep."

Riley didn't smile. "Not that quiet, mister. We've had our share of excitement. Bank was robbed yesterday."

"Brome," said Slocum.

Two drinkers close by turned to look at Slocum. "Brome —do you know him?" asked one, his eyes narrowed.

"Never met him. Just seen his work."

The men were burly, one taller, both wore vests, Levi's, and Colts in their holsters. "What work?"

"Dirty work. Back in Five Spots, he shot Selby and MacKay. Burned their places."

"What's your business in Aurora?" asked one politely.

"I'm tryin' to track that bastard down."

"What do you have in mind?"

"Make him pay for the killings."

They smiled at each other. Then the tall one said, "Well, mister, this Brome shot five men. Three were stage men. We just came in, replacements. We hear this Brome is one mean coyote. He's got three men with him, and you're trackin' him yourself. Don't you figger you're a bit outnumbered?"

"I've been outnumbered before." Slocum lifted his drink.

The men smiled. "You've got a lot of confidence."

"I expect my young pardner will be coming to help."

"Who's that?" asked Riley.

"Tad Selby. He'll be here. Appreciate it, Riley, if you tell him I'm pickin' up the Brome trail."

Riley nodded. "Think you ought to know, Sheriff Cole

and his posse has gone lickety-split after that Brome bunch. Reckon we'll be hearin' something soon."

Just then, a redhead at the top of the stairs spotted Slocum at the bar; she slowly started downstairs, her eyes fixed on him. Slocum watched her move, a fascinating rhythm. She made his groin ache. The redhead, who had a sharp eye for a keyed up customer, focused hard on the lean, powerful stranger. She sidled over to him at the bar, and smiled coquettishly.

Slocum sighed; he'd like to pierce this passion flower, but she wasn't the target. Brome was. For a moment, he wondered if the sheriff and his posse would grab Brome; then he dolefully shook his head. No small-time sheriff was going to nail a slick coyote like Brome.

"Ruby," she said, "is the name, and pleasure's the game." She moved very close. "Just the sight of a real man makes me feel bubbly inside."

He looked at the pink flesh of her breasts, part of which showed over her low-cut velvet dress, and he sighed. "Well, Ruby, I wish I had the time to give you the attention you deserve, but I'm in a hurry. Just one more whiskey, and I'm gone."

"Gone where?" She moved closer, letting her breast delicately brush up against his body.

He coughed. "Gotta track down a varmint."

Ruby shook her head. "I knew an hombre who wouldn't stop for a piece of fun, in a hurry to track down a varmint, and when he lay on his back, on his way to the next world, he cussed himself as a blasted fool for not grabbing his fun before the gunfire."

Slocum laughed and motioned Riley to pour him a last whiskey. "You're very persuading."

"I can think of a better one," she murmured, turning, and by accident, it seemed, her hand gently brushed over his crotch.

He looked at her, at her bee-stung lips, the swell of her breasts, the curve of her hips. His mind said, forget this, go for Brome, but the hardening in his britches was telling him to jump this hoyden and get the fire out of his system.

He breathed hard. He had to pick up Brome's trail. This town sheriff might need his gun. Who knew what the hell was happening out there? He just had to forget Ruby.

And Ruby, seeing her prey slipping away, turned from him, dropped her kerchief, bent to pick it up, slipping back to let her rounded buttocks rub against Slocum's fly front. His resolve melted. He felt the jump in his britches and gave up the fight.

He'd run through Ruby fast, get it out of his system, and maybe the delay would give Tad time to catch up.

8

Brome led his bunch at a hard run until he reached high ground. He found a spot with good shelter: trees, thick brush, and rocks. Sooner or later, he expected a posse in hot pursuit.

It'd be best to be tricky and lose the posse on the trail; next best, scare them by potshotting a few; if that didn't work, wipe them out. When it came to protecting stolen money, Brome was bloodthirsty. He'd spent time in Yuma prison, and he had no intention of going back; he'd choose Boot Hill instead.

They all swung off the horses, looked at each other, and grinned.

"Nice work." Brome jerked the whiskey bottle out of his saddlebag, took a long pull, and passed it. Each drank, wiping their mouths.

They sat on the rocks, drinking. Brome wiped the sweat off his forehead with his sleeve.

"That was damn good shootin', Lester." He turned to the others. "I ain't one for pattin' myself, but it was smart to put Lester in the livery for a backup. For the unexpected. See, the caper is going right, you got the money, you've closed down the bank, you're ready to ride. Then, out of nowhere come Stryker and his friends. That's Lady Bad Luck, she gets a kick out of kickin' your ass. Stryker knows we've done a job in the bank, and pulls his gun quick. But we've got good ol' Lester, our backup, he shoots their butts."

Lester ran a hand over his bald pate. "It was smart, but bloody."

"Five men shot." Dom flicked his sharp nose with his finger.

"What the hell," said Gere, "bank stealing ain't tiddly-winks."

"I prefer a clean job," said Lester. "Get the money and nobody gets hurt."

Gere shook his head. "Can't make scrambled eggs without breakin' shells."

"It can be done," Dom said. "You've done it, Brome. You told us."

Brome stroked his chin. "It happens sometimes, if your luck's good. But there's always bad traps around money."

Gere looked at the satchel. "So, what money did we get?"

Brome looked down at the trail. "They'll come after us. Don't know if it's smart to stop and count."

"We went through a lot of trouble. Let's look at it," said Gere.

Brome motioned to Dom, who leaned down, opened the satchel, and turned it upside down.

The money spilled out in bunches, big packets of bills banded together.

The men's eyes glittered.

"What d'ya think about splittin' it now?" said Lester.

Brome looked at him coldly. "Don't think much of it. Counting is a careful thing, and we've got trouble trailin' us. Best to concentrate on how to handle the posse."

"We keep runnin' till we wear 'em out or move out of their territory," said Lester.

"You won't be able to sleep nights, fearin' they'll cut your throat while you're dreamin'," Brome said.

"We try to lose them. Cross the river to wipe out our tracks," said Gere.

"We'll try that. Best not to confront them." Brome motioned to Dom, who carefully put the money back in the satchel.

Brome's brows knitted. "We'll try to get to the river before dark, cross, and hope they lose us. Then we'll go to the hut for Doc and the filly."

Gere exchanged a glance with Dom. He didn't care for that idea, but there was no avoiding it. Brome was weird about that woman. Gere wanted Doc to get his share, but the filly was the sticker. In his bones, Gere felt she'd be trouble. They were marauders, and marauders didn't lug women around; a filly was unpredictable, a fuse to set off dynamite. He'd seen it. Gere had been set against her from the beginning, but she was a thorn in Brome's side. Gere lit a cigar, and tried to mask his feelings.

But Brome had already seen something in Gere and was thinking about him. Gere was a hardnose; tough, strong, with a lot of savvy. It was good to have such an hombre in the bunch, but maybe he had too much savvy. Gere was acting leery, and Brome knew why. It had to do with Durante. Gere figured quick enough *why* Durante got shot.

Even in Yuma, before the escape, while negotiating with Durante, Brome had been ready to give him his price. He always figured one bullet would cancel the debt. He did it at Selby's, and Gere understood immediately. The others figured Brome had shot Durante because he refused an order during a caper and, at such a time, you couldn't have a failure in discipline.

Yes, Brome thought, it would pay to give Gere close attention; a man who was too savvy could be dangerous. He smiled.

"Not to worry, Gere. Everything will come up right."

Then Dom said, "Reckon we're goin' to have some guests."

Brome looked down the trail. Through his field glasses he saw eight horses, picking their way, following the trail up the slope. It was the posse.

9

Tad watched Mady doing her chores outside the house and found it pleasant. His mood, at this time, was different from a day earlier, when Slocum rode off in pursuit of the Brome bunch. Being left behind had put Tad in a rage; he hated doing nothing while Brome rode free.

Still, he came to realize that Slocum's decision had been wise; if he'd gone riding, it would have started the bleeding again, weakening him, which would have slowed Slocum down.

From the long view, it was better to rest, build his strength, and hope that he and Slocum would catch up with the Brome bunch. Because, above all, Tad wanted it to be his gun that would shoot the hell out of Brome.

So he took it easy and ate well, hoping it would speed his recovery.

He sat in the shade of the big cottonwood and brooded about Brome, itching to be up and away.

Mady fed him nourishing soup, roast beef, yams and turnip greens, and pecan pie for dessert. Living with his dad on potluck, Tad enjoyed the food and ate gluttonously of Mady's wonderful cooking. It made her smile; she liked cooking for a man, especially this vigorous, blue-eyed, handsome lad.

So he loafed, watched the horses, and stared into the horizon. And he watched Mady. She was a buxom woman with chestnut hair, and her movements were graceful. When she bent to work on her seedlings, he couldn't help notice her plush buttocks. She didn't seem to mind his looking; she'd just smile. He'd smile, too, embarrassed.

At the end of the second day, he felt his strength returning.

That night, when he was in bed and she brought a warm broth, he said, "I'm feeling better. I might ride tomorrow."

She looked at his wound thoughtfully. "I wouldn't rush. Riding can start the bleeding again. Then you'd be worse off. It's comfortable here, you'll mend quicker."

He liked looking at her pretty face. "I hate to let Slocum meet that bunch alone. They're tough hombres, and it's my fight."

She nodded. "You're right to think like that. But you wouldn't be much good if you bleed because of the riding."

She was sitting on the edge of his bed, and he smelled her female flesh. When she leaned down to pick up his soup dish, he looked into the cleavage of her bosom and could see the curve of her breast, and a glimpse of her nipple. He felt a quick flash of desire.

She straightened up, put her hand on his thigh. "You're a brave lad. You and Slocum came in my time of need." Her eyes gleamed. "Hate to think what would have happened if you hadn't been there, and those rotten dogs grabbed me."

"Killing was too good for them." Tad squirmed as he thought what they might have done to her, and that he'd complained when Slocum rode to help.

"I reckon I'm a bit selfish," she said. "I like you being here. I been a lonely lady for a long time."

"But—what about your husband?"

"Didn't have much feelin' for him, I've got to be honest."

Her hand was still on his thigh, sort of innocent. But her closeness, the sight of her breast, the memory of her buttocks as she worked outside, were doing things to him. He looked at her pretty, round face, at her gray eyes, her full mouth. Then it happened; his flesh erected under the blanket. He could see the rise in the blanket. It was a hell of a rise. It embarrassed him; he hoped she'd go before she noticed it.

And notice it she did, for her eyes widened, and she looked at him, and she smiled.

"I declare, I do believe you like me," she said.

Tad felt like sinking into the bed. He'd never had a girl; he dreamed of them, lusted after them, but he never dared to think he was ready for them.

And here he was in a bedroom, in a bed, with a lovely, buxom woman close by, smiling at his excitement. He didn't know what to do. But Mady seemed to be amused, in fact, fascinated by what had happened to him.

"Yes", she said, looking at the ponderous bump in the blanket. "You're a stalwart lad and I think you've got a craving."

He gulped, but said nothing.

She kept smiling. "If I think about it, you've done me a good turn. Saved me from violation by those rotten dogs. And here you are, suffering torments of the flesh. There's no reason why I can't show you my gratitude. Is there, Tad?"

He just stared, unable to think of anything, his erection fierce as hell.

She looked into his eyes, but her hand crept under the blanket, and gently touched his protuberance. He almost jumped, but she pressed him back to the bed. He lay there, hypnotized, like a bird by a snake, and stared at her. Her fingers snaked into his drawers and lightly began to stroke his flesh. He felt scorched. A blush had crept over the creamy skin of her face; she, too, was feeling something.

"Like a stallion," she said softly as her hand moved over and over his organ.

He was breathing hard, when she stopped.

"Just stay there," she said, and unbuttoned her dress. Within half a minute, she was nude as a jay, and his eyes were starting out of his head. He'd never seen a nude woman before, and to him, she was the most beautiful creature he'd ever laid his eyes on. He gazed at the full roundness of her breasts, the nipples, the circle around them, at her button, her rounded belly, her thighs, and the wonder between them.

She could see his amazement, and had to smile. "You've never had a woman before, Tad?"

He shook his head.

"Well, you leave it to me." She pulled back the blanket, pulled down his drawers, stared at him, and gulped. "You're more of a man than you think."

She got alongside him, turned to him, kissed his mouth,

took his arms, put them around her, pressed her body against his. He groaned with the excitement.

Then she told him to slide over her, which he did, goggle-eyed all the time. She spread her legs, took hold of him, and guided him in.

"Lordy," he said.

She took a long, deep breath. "Oh, you're something."

She held his hips over her and told him to move.

And move he did, at first slowly, as if she was a fragile thing, and he might hurt her, then he moved quicker, then frantically, then caught in an instinctive spasm, he pumped like a madman, and the thing happened, and his eyes almost popped out of his head as he felt the climax.

She flung her arms around him, and felt the waves, and her eyes shone with tears of pleasure.

She still could feel him, and smiled. "You jest stay there, Tad, rest a few minutes, then do it again, you hear?"

"I hear," he said.

And Tad spent most of that night learning the inexhaustible pleasures of making love.

The next day Tad continued to discover the fascinations of a woman's body. But the third night, he was practically sleepless, for he knew that his place was alongside Slocum, not the curvy body of a woman.

In the morning, he saddled up his pinto. Mady stood alongside, looking into his face.

"You feel strong enough to ride?"

He nodded.

She looked away, then back at him. "I hope you don't have bad thoughts about what happened."

He stared. "Bad? It was the best thing ever happened."

She looked content.

He stroked his chin. "I think I love you, Mady."

"You're young, Tad." Her face tightened. "Good luck. Be careful."

She watched him, a stalwart young man riding off to avenge the death of his family.

Riding along, Tad realized he had lost precious time with Mady, but it hadn't been his choice. He'd been stopped by an injury; while recovering, he had stumbled into something wonderful. Yes, he'd taken a side trail, but now he was headed for the target.

Tad's young face hardened and he pushed the pinto to a faster pace. Toward Aurora, Slocum, and Brome.

Through field glasses, Brome studied the posse as they started up the long slope. He smiled grimly. They were pushing their horses, in a hurry to string up the bank thieves and recover their money. Fat chance.

He had stopped on smart ground; the rocks gave good cover and it was a good position to pour down hellfire, thin out the posse. He turned to his men. "It's goin' to be like shootin' fish in a barrel."

He pulled his canteen and drank water. Gere reached for the glasses and studied the riders for a long look. "Hey, Brome, I don't see fish in a barrel."

Brome scowled and grabbed the field glasses back. The posse had stopped, and one horseman, maybe a tracker, continued up, while the others sought cover. Brome swore; they weren't dumb after all. They were sending up a scout, rather than risk the whole posse.

"A scout," Brome said. "So do we let him come or pick him off?"

"Let him come, find nothing, and bring up the rest," said Lester. "Then we hit them."

"If he's a scout, he's goin' to find something," said Dom.

"We got the money," said Gere. "If we tangle with them, there's always a chance we can lose it. Let's go for the river. Lose them there."

Brome scowled. "No guarantee we'll lose them. I don't like riding, and thinking about guns chasing me. Spoils my peace of mind. I figger we ought to clean our prints, fool this deputy so he tells 'em to keep comin'. Then we burn them."

Gere shrugged, and wondered if Brome always took a decision that exposed his men to gunfire. Maybe he figured every man who got shot gave him a fatter money split. It seemed foolish, because there were only four of them and surely Brome needed every gun.

They cut branches and went over their prints, smoothing them out. Dom moved the horses into the trees, out of sight, while the men took positions behind the rocks and thick brush.

They waited, and the sun broiled down.

Gere, crouched behind a crag, felt it burn his back. He sweated. If the deputy was sharp-eyed he'd pick up the smoothed-out prints. Then, it'd be a standoff; he wouldn't send the posse a signal. What then? They'd shoot the scout and ride for the river, which he had suggested in the first place. That's how you stop the posse. You could hit them bogged down in the river, too. That's hitting fish in a barrel.

Time dragged and Gere wondered what the hell was keeping the scout. Well, he wouldn't be eager to come over the edge, that'd be the moment of truth.

Gere's thoughts returned to Brome. Why had he stepped in to knock out the horse thief, then shoot the Mexican? He used his superfast draw. "There isn't time," Brome had said. Gere thought about that. Maybe he wanted the bunch intact until *after* the bank job. But now there was money to split, and if you lost a man, the split would be fatter. Now was the time to keep a hard eye on Brome.

A soft sound interrupted Gere's flow of thought. He saw Brome hold up his hand and point.

The men watched the edge of the slope, but nothing happened. In the silence, the sun glared, a buzzard soared high in the sky, a warm breeze brushed Gere's cheek.

Then a rock sailed over the edge, bounced off a big crag and slithered. The Brome bunch held fast; it was a trick, to startle a man, make him fire his gun.

Finally, over the edge, the top of a man's head appeared, his dark eyes swiveling, looking. Silence. He was listening. Then all of him came up. A wiry cowboy, stubble-bearded, gun in hand. He paused at the edge, looked down, then moved forward. What grabbed him were the tracks left by Dom riding the horses toward the trees. He stood thinking, and for a breathless moment let his eyes circle the terrain. Then he walked to the slope edge and his arm swept up. He pulled a plug of tobacco from his pocket and bit a chew.

It was tough, Gere thought, lying there, almost not breathing, as the posse started to climb. He could hear them. Sweat trickled on Gere's neck. He peered toward Brome. Why in hell wait? It'd be dangerous if the posse reached the top; best to hit them as they climbed, they'd be sitting ducks.

Just then, the scout looked suspiciously at the ground, at the smoothed-out prints, and his head jerked. He brought his gun up, searching for bushwhackers, ready to fire to warn the men below. But Brome, who had never let his eyes stray from the scout, fired, and the man plummeted back and dropped like a stone.

The bunch ran to the edge and crouched. Below, the men of the posse, warned by the shot, jerked at the reins, swung off their saddles, and tried to dash for the sparse rock cover.

Brome fired fast and his heavy bullets tore two men stumbling toward a half-buried rock. They fell and sprawled. Lester and Gere each fired at two burly deputies, slow to reach the heavy brush. They fell, twisted, and lay still. The others, from the safety of cover, sent up a barrage of bullets.

Brome, flat on his stomach, peering down the slope, felt they'd done enough damage. A posse reduced to four men was not threatening.

At the first sound of gunfire, Dom had started the horses on a run toward the slope.

The men fired a few more bullets to keep the posse pinned down, then ran to meet Dom, swinging into their saddles.

They looked at each other.

Brome was grinning. "A little bloodletting always slows down the law."

"Not only the law," said Gere, his face grim.

"There's only four men now; reckon they'll keep comin'?" asked Lester.

"They'll keep comin'," said Dom quietly.

"Why?" Brome looked curiously at Dom.

"'Cause we got forty thousand dollars belonging to that town. And no sheriff is goin' back to that banker with four men still sitting on their horses."

"Reckon so." Brome smiled.

"We can try to lose them at the river," said Gere.

"We'll hit them in the river," said Brome. "That's best in the long run."

Brome put his horse into a hard gallop, and the men followed close behind.

The sun had slipped lower in the sky, and to Gere it seemed the air had cooled.

10

Slocum came out of Riley's Saloon a happier man. Ruby had satisfied the cravings of his flesh. But it slowed his pursuit of Brome, and he felt the prick of conscience. The appetites of a man sure could do a lot of damage, he thought.

Under a brittle blue sky with lazy, lacy clouds, he walked his horse on the dry red dirt of the town. He went past the general store, the cafe, the livery. A workman was fixing the splintered window of the Aurora bank.

Slocum dismounted and went into the bank.

The manager was sitting at his desk, writing. He had a fleshy face, iron gray hair, and bit on an unlit cigar; he looked mean. Slocum walked over and read A. E. Stiller on the wooden plaque. He stood there, waiting for Stiller to stop writing and look up. He did neither.

After a full minute, Stiller said gruffly, "Yes, what is it?"

"I heard that Brome hit your bank. Hard."

Stiller's hand stopped as if paralyzed, his eyes swiveled to the lean, green-eyed, powerful stranger wearing a Colt with a worn handle.

"Hard enough. Your name?"

"Slocum. John Slocum."

Stiller's body half turned. "Do you know Brome?"

"Not personally. Hope to meet him soon. But I know something he did."

"What'd he do?"

"Bad killings back in the town of Five Spots."

"He did bad killings here, too. And cleaned out the bank."

Stiller waited, but the stranger said nothing. "So you've come to tell me you know Brome, is that it?"

Slocum didn't smile. "Who knows? Maybe I'll get your money back."

Stiller looked grim. "I've got the sheriff and a posse out there, doing that. I hope." Stiller chewed his lip. "Is it just you hunting Brome? Those who have seen him shoot say he's the fastest gun in this territory. He's a murdering, mean, heartless killer. You talk like a brave man, but reckless."

Then Stiller looked into the piercing green eyes of the stranger and felt squirmy. Whoever this son of a bitch was, he sure generated power. His look was like the kick of a stallion. Stiller felt he had been patronizing and regretted it.

"All I want from you is a description of Brome," Slocum said quietly.

Stiller put down his pen, aware that Slocum was trailing a man he'd never seen. And that he'd come to get a description from someone who'd been practically nose to nose with Brome.

"I'm sorry if I was abrupt. If you lose forty thousand

dollars, you don't ooze goodness and light." He stopped to visualize Brome. "He wears a short-brimmed black hat, yellow vest, and checked shirt. He's got a broad face, thick bones, gray pitted eyes. He's not big, all sinews, that's why he's fast. And he looks dangerous. I should have listened to my instinct. But I've met men who look like they couldn't afford a square meal and they deposit thousands of dollars. Yeah, I should have listened to my instinct about Brome."

Slocum smiled as he turned to go. "Maybe it worked out for the best, Mr. Stiller. You're still breathin'."

Stiller stared. "Barely. Every time I think of the money, my heart stops." He looked toward the door. "Sheriff Cole is sure taking a long time. It's worrisome."

He watched Slocum with his lean, catlike gait, walk out of the door.

Stiller stared into space.

11

Sheriff Cole looked at the graves, his face grim. He had sent his deputy, Mac, up the slope to make sure all was clear on top. He had trusted him, trusted the wrong man. A deadly mistake. Now Mac was in the grave with the other men who had been shot in ambush.

When they brought the bodies up the slope, they found Mac shot, lying on his face.

Sheriff Cole looked at the earth carefully and when he discovered the smoothed-out prints, he ground his teeth.

"Look here, Todd," he spoke to his heavy-jawed, husky deputy. "These coyotes tried to cover their prints. And Mac missed it. It cost him."

Todd looked at the ground. "Cost us, too, sheriff. We can't afford that. We got hit like sitting ducks."

"This Brome is a smart bastard. They're a cagey bunch." The sheriff's slate-blue eyes stared in the distance, as if hoping he could see them. "We're cut in half. So now they're four and we're four."

The men looked at him. Then Olaf said, "They're rough, sheriff. Reckon it would be better if we went back and built up the posse?"

The sheriff stared at him. "Go back? We can't do that."

"Why not?"

"Stiller wouldn't stop screamin'. He'd say we let these coyotes get out too far, that we won't ever catch them. And he might be right."

"They robbed our bank, killed our boys. We owe them a hanging," said Todd.

"Damn right," agreed Gibson.

Sheriff Cole took off his hat and scratched his head. The sun was lower in the sky, three hours before sundown. There could be no turning back. He looked at his men, tough and strong. He had to press forward, get that rotten gang, track them, shoot them, lynch them. He'd done it before, with the Grady bunch, also a vicious gang. The main thing was surprise. To creep up on them and pour on the lead. Yes, he'd follow the Brome bunch to hell and back, and find the right time to hit them. He'd bring back the money, and be the town hero.

He put on his hat, his square, tanned face resolute. "If we get the money, Stiller will show his gratitude to each man. Let's go for this rotten bunch. We owe Brome a hangin'."

They grinned, mounted up, and started tracking.

Just before sundown, when the sky was blazing orange and red, they reached the river. The sheriff stopped to think. That Brome bunch had gone straight for the river, but you'd expect that; Brome was not dumb, whatever else he might be.

The river flowed quietly, slowly, as if nothing could disturb its calm. It would take about ten minutes to cross. The Brome tracks went into the river, four horses. Where did their tracks come out? Downstream or directly across? The other side had rocks, thick brush, and shrubbery nourished by the water.

Sheriff Cole pondered. Should they cross now or wait till dark? Waiting was safer. But what if they were not lurking in that shrubbery? There would be time lost. They might never catch up. If they crossed now, anything could happen. Brome was sly, he could be there.

The men were looking at him, waiting impatiently; he couldn't stand here with his finger up his ass; he had to do something. He himself didn't like crossing now, but they were itching to move, especially Gibson, who had lost his brother at the slope.

"Okay, men, what d'ya think?"

Gibson spoke quickly. "I think we're wastin' time. Let's get those dogs and string 'em up. We ain't goin' to do it standing here."

The sheriff rubbed his lips with his finger. "They might be waitin' for us to get in the water, Gibson."

"I don't see that," said Olaf. "They've got a lotta money, why would they hang around?"

"They waited before," said the sheriff.

"Yeah, but we were right on their tails then," said Todd. "After they bloodied us, they figgered we slunk on home."

"You get in that water, and if they're waitin', you're a dead duck," said the sheriff.

"I think they're runnin'. They've got money to spend," said Todd.

"I gotta go ahead, sheriff, no matter what," said Gibson

through clenched teeth. "They shot my brother; I gotta have blood."

He started for the river, followed by Todd and Olaf.

The sheriff didn't like it. He sat there, thinking they should wait till dark. He watched them in the river, then he thought he should be out front, leading them. But before starting, he stared across the river and caught the glint of light on metal. His flesh crawled.

"Ambush!" he yelled, grabbing his rifle, and diving toward cover. But they were already in the river.

His cry started the crackle of gunfire from the shrubbery on the other bank.

Sheriff Cole blanched as the barrage hit. The horses screamed, twisted, and the river boiled. The men were cut down. They slid out of their saddles into the river. The current carried them downstream, and for a while their heads bobbed; then there was just the water.

From behind a crag, the sheriff peered out, his face racked with anguish. There was blood in the stream and though the air was cool, he felt sweat on his forehead.

In two ambushes, the Brome bunch had wiped out the posse.

He stayed crouched behind the rock, cradling his rifle. The dark slipped down quickly, and from the other bank, he heard the dim sound of voices carried on the breeze. They wouldn't care about one survivor. What could he do?

Sheriff Cole bit his lip in fury. The whole thing was a disaster. He had botched it; he should have taken command. He had known Brome was sly, tricky. Such a man would decide on ambush at the river. He cursed himself for letting the men ride. But could he have stopped them? Gibson was in a rage about his brother. Todd was sure he was right.

That Brome bunch were mean and smart bastards. They outfoxed him.

Now he'd have to go back. He dreaded it. Seven dead men. And in town, five men had been shot. The Brome bunch was untouched and they still had the money.

A disaster. Sheriff Cole crouched behind the rock. He felt misery in his bones. Soon he'd start back toward Aurora.

Brome looked at the horses in the river, struggling to reach the shore. The heads of the riders were no longer visible; they had floated downstream. "Well, that tears them up," he said.

"There's one hiding on the riverbank," said Dom.

"He can live or die," Brome said.

The men pulled out the whiskey bottle and drank.

Gere looked thoughtfully at the satchel of money near Dom. "Now that we're through with them, we can concentrate on the money," he said. "Might be a good time for the split."

Brome shook his head. "Never saw a man in a greater hurry about splittin' the take."

Gere's smile was a little forced. "Money in your pockets is a nice feeling, Brome."

"Yeah, a good feelin'. But what about Doc? He's part of the split. We could wait till we get to the hut."

"Doc? He wasn't in this party," said Gere.

"You don't think so? I think so."

Gere looked at the other men before he spoke.

"Guarding *your* woman, Brome?"

Brome shrugged. "You got me wrong, Gere. I ain't greedy 'bout her."

"A beautiful filly like that? I thought you'd hog her."

"Naw. I used to have special feelings. But after what she did, you can all take a piece."

The men looked at each other, and thought of Belle, a beautiful, buxom filly. They grinned.

"Ready to ride now?" Brome asked.

"What about the last of the posse?" said Lester.

"To hell with him. He can't do anything." Brome's smile was evil. "He was smart enough not to get in the river. A man like that deserves to live a bit longer."

Brome looked west and licked his lips. "Now, let's ride to the hut and see what's happening to our Belle."

Slocum pulled up on the roan and mopped his brow. Though it was past midday, the sun still burned fiercely in a hot, blue sky. His mind, however, was not on the heat but on the four graves that had been dug alongside the trail. He studied the earth and shook his head.

Four men in the posse shot. They had run into a barrage of bullets and gone down, like lambs to slaughter. Brome and his guns had been sitting on the slope and waiting. Slocum stood there, silent, thinking. Though half the posse had been mowed down, they continued to track Brome.

That sheriff wasn't too bright. He didn't seem to get the idea he was tracking a fox. The more Slocum learned, the more he realized that Brome was a trickster. He sure outsmarted the bank guards and, when he got out here, he outfoxed the posse.

Who the hell was Brome? Where'd he come from? You'd expect an outlaw like him to have a rep in this territory. But Slocum had heard nothing of Brome.

He became aware of a movement far down the trail, a solitary figure riding toward him. He studied the rider through his field glasses. A big man, slumped in his saddle and wearing a star. The sheriff, alone, on the trail back. Slocum's jaw hardened. The one survivor; why else would he be riding alone, so downhearted?

Slocum lit a cigarillo and waited.

By the time the sheriff reached Slocum he had straightened up. He didn't know what to make of this stranger. He didn't look threatening and couldn't belong to Brome's bunch; they were behind him. The sheriff stayed alert.

"Reckon you didn't have much luck with Brome," the stranger drawled.

Sheriff Cole studied the strong, green-eyed man leaning against the saddle of his roan. "Who are you, mister?"

"Slocum's the name. I been riding your trail."

"And why were you doing that?"

"I had a little talk with Stiller. I'm ridin' Brome's trail, too."

"Why?"

"After his hide, sheriff."

Sheriff Cole looked carefully at Slocum, the rugged face, the steady green eyes, the powerful body, the smooth handle of his gun. He decided not to laugh.

"Are you alone?"

Slocum nodded.

The sheriff rubbed his chin. "I lost seven men to that bunch. Does that tell you something about Brome?"

"A foxy bastard."

"I figure you'll need help."

"I'd like to have help, sheriff, but I gotta go with what I've got."

"You hunting him for the reward?"

"Personal reasons."

"Well, Slocum, you better be the smartest tracker in the territory and the fastest gun. 'Cause you're bucking one helluva bunch."

"I figger that."

"They hit us at the river," the sheriff said, his eyes squinting. "The boys were thirsty for blood. They wouldn't wait till dark. They got caught in the river. I wasn't ready for the river. Saved me."

"Sheriff, you did the smart thing. What now?"

"Don't know. Goin' back. But it doesn't look good."

Slocum climbed into the saddle. "Reckon I'll ride on, sheriff."

The sheriff stood and watched him ride, and after a few minutes, looked down at his star, wrenched it from his chest, and flung it into the brush. He nudged his horse toward Aurora.

A few hours later, Slocum picked up movement on the trail behind him.

He had been following the Brome bunch and the tracks were old; he should be moving faster. But he had pushed the roan to the limit and he was not going to ruin that precious animal, no matter what.

He decided to test who the rider was following, so he took a turn off Brome's trail and rode for a time. Through field glasses, he looked back at the rider, watched him stop, as if puzzled, then take the turnoff. Slocum smiled, lit a cigarillo, and waited. The tracker was following him, not Brome.

When Tad came in sight, he studied the tanned, strong young face. Maybe it was his imagination, but there was something different in it. Slocum smiled, wondering if Tad had grown up a bit during his stay with Mady. Good thing. Nothing more tragic, in Slocum's view, than for a cowboy, eager for revenge, to end prematurely in Boot Hill before tasting the major pleasures of this world.

"How'd it go, Tad?"

Tad swung off his pinto, his face grim. He gave the horse a handful of grain and patted him. "I practically killed this horse trying to catch up with you, Slocum."

"I didn't travel that fast. Brome is two days ahead of us."

Tad took off his hat and mopped his brow. "Why'd you turn off Brome's trail back there?"

"Had to know if it was me being tailed or Brome. When you took my trail, I figured it might be you."

Tad's blue eyes squinted at a long view of rocky hills and valleys over which cloud shadows raced. His keen young eyes searched the land for the movement of man, but he saw none.

Slocum noticed that Tad had lost his paleness; his face looked ruddy and strong.

"You look okay. Mady patched you up pretty good."

Tad looked sharply at Slocum. "Reckon it was smart to wait a couple of days after all. You were right."

Slocum repressed a smile and said nothing.

"I'm goin' to marry her," Tad said.

Slocum was startled. That was the way with a young-blood. The first woman he nailed, he was ready to die for. That was nature. Tad had to do some growing up before he could think of marriage. And in his deadly quest for Brome, there was little guarantee that Tad would live long enough to taste the uncertain pleasures of life with Mady. What did you tell a kid like this?

"First things first, Tad. We're trailin' a tough bunch."

"They're cowardly skunks," Tad grated.

"But they're dangerous. They held up the bank in Aurora; shot five men there. Then they wiped out the posse; seven men."

Tad's jaw hardened. "They should be drawn and quartered."

Slocum looked at the sky, intense blue, with lazy floating clouds, and in the distance the saw-toothed mountains were sharp in the dazzling light of the sun.

He glanced at Tad; the kid had a secret smile. What the hell was he thinking of?

"Only reason I tell you this, Tad, I want you to keep your mind focused hard on Brome. You can't ride around with dreams of Mady. If you lose your concentration, you won't see Mady or any other filly again."

Tad scowled, then remembered his father and his kid brother, and a gust of fury swept through him. Slocum was right. Start thinking of women, of fun on the blankets, and your brain went woozy. You'd forget what you were riding for.

"Glad you reminded me, Slocum. There's only one thing I'm living for. And that's to kill Brome."

Slocum nodded, and swung onto the roan.

They started to ride, picking up Brome's trail. It seemed headed for the hills, not for any town. That was curious. Was he going to lie low? They had the money, and maybe they wanted a quiet place to split it.

12

Belle sat in the rickety old chair, resting against the back of the hut, and watched Doc Edwards as he curried his horse, a buckskin. He was tender with the animal, and every so often his strong hands rubbed the nose of the horse.

She had been locked up with Doc for two days, though it seemed forever. And each moment now, she was expecting, with a clutch of fear at her heart, that Brome would ride into view. She pictured that moment and dreaded it, just as she had dreaded the moment when Brome had burst into the ranch house where she lived with MacKay. The sight of Brome at her threshold with a gun, his face in a hard sneer, had filled her with horror.

That was curious because, in the old days, she'd been fascinated by Brome, thought him manly and strong. But that was before Yuma, before she discovered the dark side of Brome. It happened two years ago when, drunk and vicious, Brome had slugged Selby.

In those days, they'd all been younger, and in bad shape. They fell in together after the war; Brome, Selby, MacKay —broke and desperate. She knew MacKay and Selby, and was with them when Brome cooked up his scheme for robbing the Dawson bank.

It'd be a one-shot job. If it worked, they'd go straight, buy ranches, raise cattle, settle down, and stay clear of the law. Selby needed money for his motherless two boys, cared for by his aunt.

Belle had been friendly with all the men, favoring Selby a bit. They were not criminals, just desperate, hungry men.

So they did the job, clever and clean. Nobody got hurt, and they came away from the bank with twenty thousand; a dream come true. In the hideaway, they began to drink, to celebrate. And Selby made his pitch to Belle; he needed someone to take care of his orphaned kids. She liked him best then, and said maybe. MacKay was disappointed, but he handled it. Brome, however, blew his cork. For some reason, he felt betrayed. Drunk as a lord, he went haywire, hit Selby with his fists and his gun butt, knocking him cold. Mac and Belle watched in horror.

Brome kept drinking afterward, as if ashamed. He drank until he passed out.

They brought Selby around and decided to leave Brome. They split the money three ways, left the unconscious Brome his share, and rode off.

That was the last they saw of him.

Later, they heard the law had nailed him in that hideaway; the sheriff brought him to Phoenix and Brome got nine years at the Yuma Penitentiary. At the trial, he didn't betray them. Now she knew why.

She had ended up living with MacKay, not Selby. It was

a quiet, contented life until Brome broke out of Yuma. He wanted revenge. He believed they had betrayed him to the law and stolen his share of the money. He killed MacKay, and told her that he'd killed Selby, too.

Belle clenched her teeth. She was convinced that Brome was loco.

He had gone off with his bunch to do a job on a bank; she heard them talking. They didn't hide anything from her. What did they fear? And he'd be back. She dreaded that.

From the moment he left, she kept wondering how to escape.

She studied Doc, a strange critter, a cool, remote man. He was built broad and muscular, with dark, piercing eyes; he looked like nothing that happened could surprise him.

The first night he told her, "Don't try anything. Brome told me if you did, to shoot. And shoot where it'd hurt you a lot, but not kill you. You understand?"

Doc didn't smile. He never smiled. He went on. "Brome sprung me outta Yuma prison. I owe him plenty. He told me to take care that you stay put. That if you gave me any trouble, to hurt you." Doc's lips twisted in an odd way; maybe he was smiling. "I'd do that. You should know." He cooked food at the fire, but didn't sit with her. Though he kept distant, she felt he always knew where she was, what she was doing.

Brome had left Doc to guard her because he was incorruptible. But she had to try. He was a man, after all. And most men thought her beautiful. She had to try something. Sooner or later she expected, he'd get bored and want company. She had to link up with him; time was running out. Once Brome got back, all would go down the drain. Brome was merciless.

It was this night, it seemed, that Doc had become restless. After he gave her dinner, he sat nearby, as if he was bored, and might like conversation. But he didn't start, he just sat near, glanced at her once, drank coffee, and looked at the night sky. There was no moon, just stars.

She sipped at her coffee; finally she spoke. "What put you in Yuma?"

His head turned slowly toward her, his lips twisted. "I shot a man in a fight."

She looked puzzled. "They jailed you for that?"

He took his time to speak. "His friends claimed he didn't have a gun at the time. But he did. The jury believed his friends."

"Then you were wrongfully imprisoned?"

"Wrongfully, yes. They gave me life."

"They gave you life. For a crime you didn't commit?"

"That's right."

"That's terrible," she said.

"Bad enough."

"Then you're not a criminal."

He looked away, then back at her. "Oh, I'm a criminal. I've held up stages, shot men, did other bad things."

"Ah," she said. That was a disappointment. For a moment she had thought him an honest citizen who might feel sympathy for her situation. But he was the same breed as Brome.

He put his horse in the back of the hut with hers, and she feared the conversation had ended. But he came back, sat near, and poured more coffee in his cup. He looked down the trail, as if searching for riders.

"You expect them soon?"

He nodded. "Soon enough. Doesn't take long."

"To rob a bank?"

He nodded grimly. "Brome's good at that."

"How would you know?"

"I was locked up with him in Yuma. He talked a lot." Doc's dark eyes glowed. "He told me all about you, Selby, and MacKay."

Her breast heaved. "He told you that we stole his share of the money?"

"Not only that."

"That we put the sheriff on him?"

Doc nodded. "A dirty trick."

"Suppose I told you, on my word of honor, that we didn't do that."

"Your word of honor. You have honor?" He looked into the fire.

She bit her lip. "Doc, you sound like a man of sense. I think Brome can go crazy. I've seen it. You haven't. I tell you before God that we left his money with him that night. That we never put the law on him." She looked into his eyes.

"So what?"

"I'm telling you, Brome is loco. I'm innocent. He hated Selby and MacKay. But they did nothing to him. He killed them. He'll kill me, too. Or do something worse. I'd rather be dead than let him do what he wants. If you give me a knife, I'll kill myself. Now."

Doc studied her. "You'd do that?"

"Try me."

He looked thoughtful. "I know Brome. He'll use you. He won't kill you. But he'll kill something in you."

"I'd rather be dead," she said.

He looked into the fire. Then he shrugged. "You see my

problem. I would be in Yuma prison now. The rest of my life. Prison is slow dying for a man. But I'm free. Free because of Brome. He took me with him when he broke out. Then he gave me a job to do. To keep you. How can I cross a man who has done that for me?"

Her heart sank.

She looked at him, and he looked at her with flat eyes, without feelings.

She opened her dress and showed her breasts.

"Take me. Take my body. But give me the chance to get away from Brome."

He looked at her breasts and his eyes glittered. He came toward her, and she felt a spark of hope. When he got close, he slapped her face hard. Then he smiled and she realized now why he did not smile. It was a horrible grimace.

"Why did Brome leave me with you, instead of the others, do you reckon? Because I can't have sex. I been ruined in the war. And when a woman tries to excite me, all it does is fill me with hate."

He stared at her. "A beautiful woman. But I don't feel a thing. It's all wasted."

He turned away and walked toward the hut. She heard him inside opening the whiskey bottle.

She shut her eyes and felt despair. She'd have to wait until Brome came, a vicious killer. She knew what he had in mind. If only she could get away. She had to try. Doc was drinking; it would dull his senses.

She moved a bit, so that he could hear her. Then, silently, she slipped to the side of the hut where the grass was thick and she could move noiselessly. It was dark, no moon, only the dim starlight. She took her shoes off, and moved into the thick shrubbery, then through it, and circled in a big arc, coming finally, in silence, to the back of the hut, where the horses were. She saddled Doc's buckskin and waited.

Doc kept drinking, and much time passed before he realized that he hadn't heard her. He came out of the hut, holding his whiskey glass, but he didn't see her; he thought she would be sitting at the fire. He looked and listened. Then he stiffened. He bent to look for her tracks. It was hard to see. She'd gone into the thickets. What the hell was she doing? Did she dream she could escape? A nuisance. He cursed and threw the glass, and went into the shrubbery, searching.

Now! She unknotted the reins from the post. She slipped onto the buckskin's back, grabbed the reins of her horse, and started to ride west, kicking hard at the buckskin's flanks.

Doc was deep in the shrubbery, thinking she was hiding somewhere in it, when he heard the horses and came running.

"Stop!" he yelled. "I'll shoot."

But she was kicking at the horse. She felt the bullet whistle over her head, then the crackle of gunfire; more bullets. It was dark. Was he aiming or shooting blind? It didn't matter. She was running free, with both horses. She'd ride all night long to get away. Brome would be back, and soon. Oh, he'd trail her. He wouldn't let her go. He was vicious, he wanted revenge. She'd ride all night if she had to, till she reached Dodson, or someone, somewhere.

The burden that had lain over her heart was gone. Now she had a fighting chance.

Doc sat on a crag and stared at the mountains in the distance, but he didn't see them. He had drunk a lot of whiskey, but still didn't feel drunk. He wouldn't feel drunk now if he drank a barrel. The worst thing he could imagine had happened: Belle had escaped.

Before he had left, Brome, with his gray pitted eyes staring, had told him: "Stay close to her, Doc. She'll try to get away. She'll try everything. Tell her if she tries, you'll kill her." Brome put his hand on his shoulder. "You see how I feel about it, Doc?"

"Don't worry, Brome."

So after they rode toward Aurora, Doc had told her, "Don't try to escape, don't make trouble or I'll kill you." And that tamed her. He believed that. She moped around. He believed she didn't have the nerve to run. He knew plenty about Belle. In prison he and Brome were cellmates, and you got close to your cellmate. Brome thought about women a lot; men did that in prison. But he, Doc, didn't think about women. He had told Brome he'd been hit in the war; it damaged a nerve and it finished him for sex.

Brome didn't laugh like the others. Brome had told him that in prison a man was tortured by sex dreams, that as long as he was locked up in Yuma, he'd be glad to change places with Doc. And he talked about Belle, a betraying bitch, how he hated her, and that when he got out, he'd make her pay. Her and those two treacherous coyotes, Selby and MacKay.

It was Brome's hate, his thirst for revenge, that kept his spirits up in Yuma. When a chance for the breakout came, Brome picked Doc to go, with the others. He was there with Brome when he came down on Selby and MacKay—a whirlwind of fire and blood.

And what Brome had dreamed in Yuma had come true—Belle. He grabbed her, too. And Brome had trusted him to guard the woman while they went to break the bank in

Aurora. It hadn't been a big thing to ask: Keep an eye on the woman.

All had gone well as long as Doc kept his distance from Belle. It came apart when he got itchy and started to talk to her. And she had told him she was innocent; that Brome had killed two men who did nothing to him. Was she lying? No, he didn't think so. So who took the money, and told the sheriff who picked up Brome?

What would Brome do? He was shrewd, but a bit loco. Doc gritted his teeth. It could go either way. He might be able to ride it out. But he had failed Brome. Durante, too, had botched up. He was six feet under.

Doc grimaced: Even if he wanted to run he couldn't; she had taken his horse.

Well, he'd drink some more, and let it happen, whatever.

13

As he rode in front of his men toward the hideaway, Brome felt good. Things were going nicely: He had done the bank job and come away with forty thousand dollars; he had wiped out the posse. What remained was to divvy the money. And Belle.

Belle—he had thought about her every day he spent rotting in Yuma; in his mind he pictured some things he'd do if ever he got hold of her. The pictures were not nice.

He had paid off Selby and MacKay, burned them out of his system.

Now it was her turn. A proud bitch, but he knew how to humble her. When he got through, she'd be a worn-out dishrag. He knew how to wipe out that high-and-mighty look in her eyes.

They were nearing the hideaway. He could see steep bluffs in the distance, and nearby were the narrow-leaved trees of the high country.

Five miles north, his brother Seth lived on a small homestead with his wife Millie. He owed them a visit, but only after he took care of what he had in mind.

An hour more of riding brought them in sight of the hideaway. The closer he came to Belle, the more Brome felt the excitement.

As they rode toward the hut, they saw Doc come out, holding a glass of whiskey. Something was different about Doc; Brome could tell. His jaw clamped, he sensed misfortune, he could breathe it. But he didn't want to think it, yet.

The men swung off their horses and smiled at Doc. He stood calmly, his eyes woozy from whiskey.

"Hey, Doc," Gere said, "you're goin' to be a rich man." Gere was exhilarated. He was thinking that everything went smoothly, that they were richer now than when they left this hideaway a week ago. They were on the edge of divvying the money. And no guns were in pursuit, not anymore.

Doc's voice was low. "How rich?"

Gere stared in his eyes. "We've got forty thousand dollars to split among five men, that's how rich."

Doc just lifted his glass and drank.

Dom looked at him. "What the hell's wrong, Doc?"

"She's gone, isn't she?" said Brome.

"She's gone," said Doc.

A red flush started on Brome's neck. He took a deep breath.

There was dead silence. Gere glanced at Brome; he knew what that meant.

"Is she dead?" asked Brome.

Doc shook his head.

"Did *you* get funny?" Brome's voice grated.

Doc shook his head. "You know better, Brome."

"Did she?"

"She tried," Doc nodded.

Brome's eyes glittered. "She did? See, she's a slut." He jerked his hat off and mopped his brow. The men were silent. Then Brome pulled a bottle from his saddlebag and took a long pull. "What happened?"

"She made a pitch. Said you were wrong."

"Wrong? 'Bout what?"

"On the Abilene bank job. She said they didn't call the law, and they didn't take your money."

Brome's voice was husky. "What the hell did you expect her to say? She wanted your help to get out. Maybe she got it, Doc." Brome's gaze was piercing.

Doc shook his head. "I told her I'd kill her if she tried to escape. She was careful."

"But she got away? How long ago?"

"It's been five hours."

Brome's face was carved of stone. He raised his whiskey bottle and drank. The men watched him silently.

"So what happened?"

Doc was calm. "She showed her body, trying to get me. I slapped her. Then I went into the hut for whiskey. She was gone when I came out. She had sneaked into the shrubs. I went in. She'd been there, but made a big circle and came out behind the hut to the horses. I s'pose I should have watched them more closely, but I didn't think she'd try, after I said I'd kill her if she tried anything. She got off with both horses. I threw bullets at her, but it was dark." He bit his lip. "I'm sorry, Brome."

Brome's voice was almost gentle. "I'm sorrier, Doc. We went through a lot to get the money. We shot the posse.

We figgered a share for you. Looks like that won't happen."

Doc's face was calm. "You can penalize me. I don't want the money."

"It's more than that," said Brome. He backed off, facing Doc. The men, aware of what was in Brome's mind, all stepped back.

"More?" said Doc, understanding, but not ready.

"Pull your gun, Doc," Brome said pleasantly.

"Why?"

"I got you out of Yuma, Doc. You were there for life. I gave you a simple job. To hang on to a little chit of a woman. You screwed up."

"A man can make a mistake."

"Only if you're dumb."

The men watched Brome, fascinated.

"I'm givin' you a chance. Pull your gun."

"Not much of a chance, Brome, considering the way you draw." Doc's voice was measured.

"You gotta pay, Doc." Brome's eyes were icy. "Draw!"

Doc's eyes went dead. He knew he was finished. But he grabbed for his gun and it seemed that Brome actually watched him for a couple of beats before he moved. His bullet hit Doc in the center of his forehead, and he catapulted back, dead before he hit the ground.

Brome looked at each of the men, to see how they took it. "He screwed up. He lost the woman. He had to pay."

Gere rubbed his chin. "But you haven't lost the woman, Brome. You know that."

Brome grimaced. "Yes. We'll track her and find her."

"You knew that. Why'd you shoot Doc?" asked Dom.

"Because he screwed up. We can't carry screwups. The

bunch is in danger from a man like that." He slipped his gun into his holster. "We'll split his share."

Gere's eyes glinted. There it was again. Brome liked to shoot someone and fatten the share. He had done it with Durante; now Doc. You didn't like it when he killed a man in the bunch, but you liked it if it increased your share of the take. A neat trick.

Nobody ever said that Brome was dumb.

Gere wondered if that trick could be a danger, ultimately, to each of them.

Lester and Dom buried Doc, and afterward the men stood bareheaded at his grave for just a moment.

Brome's face was stony. He could tell the men didn't like what he'd done, but he wasn't worried. He had needed them for his revenge, for the bank, for the posse. Now they weren't important. He felt a bit uneasy about Gere, but could settle with him, if it came to that.

Still, Brome figured, it'd be foolish to break the bunch; you never knew when you'd need backup. He was an escaped felon, a wanted man in the territory. Bounty men could be looking for him right now.

It was smart to have backup. And he wanted the men for Belle, to humiliate her. He wanted her to be used as a prostitute by jailbirds; that should break her spirit.

Gere bent down and tossed some dirt over the grave. "Doc was a good ol' dog."

"Yeah," said Brome. "We got real close in prison. I liked Doc."

Gere looked at him. "You liked him? And you shot him."

Brome nodded. "That's how it goes, Gere. Sometimes you're forced to shoot your own sidekick." His broad face

hardened. "Doc let Belle get away. I probably woulda for-
given Doc anything but that. I want that woman real bad.
Maybe it was a mistake not to take care of her before we
did the bank job. But I wanted to make you boys happy.
Now she's gone."

"You won't lose her, Brome."

"You never can be sure. But we'll track her, wherever
she goes."

"What'd she do to you?" asked Lester.

Brome scowled. "I tole you. She's a Delilah. Beautiful
and two-faced, she'd sell your soul for a dime." He drank
from his whiskey bottle and wiped his mouth. "I feel bad
about Doc, but he let her get away. Couldn't forgive that.
And in Yuma I was closer to Doc than any of you."

They were silent.

"She rode west. I figure she's headed for Dodson,"
Brome said.

Gere ground his heel into the earth. The last thing he
wanted was to ride again after the grueling time they'd gone
through. He was interested in the money split.

"Brome," he said, "we've been in the saddle for a long
time. We could use a layover."

Brome's pitted eyes gleamed as he looked at the men.
"No hurry. We'll catch her. It's too bad, because if we had
Belle, we'd be enjoyin' ourselves. Even if I hate her, she's
a fine piece of woman. Bad thing Doc let her get away.
Right, Dom?"

Dom looked at the money satchel. "Tell you the truth,
Brome. I like the sight of gold more than the sight of a
woman."

Gere laughed. "Plenty of women to be had for a bit of
gold."

Lester smiled. "Let's keep our eye on the target—the money."

"Yeah." Brome suddenly seemed uninterested. He looked at the sky. It was sundown and the sky was a giant splash of primrose and orange. "Go ahead, Dom, split it four ways."

Dom grinned ear to ear. "That's music to my ears."

Lester got his whiskey bottle while Dom took the satchel from his horse and emptied it. They drank while the money was counted and split in four equal piles.

Brome seemed bored by the counting, but the other men looked at the money with shining eyes.

Gere was astonished at Brome's lack of interest. He wondered if it was a pose. The more Gere studied Brome, the more complicated he seemed to be. Not an easy man to know.

The men put their shares in their saddlebags. They were in good spirits as they sat around the fire, eating dinner.

"We'll take it easy, stay the night," Brome said. "Tomorrow we'll pick up Belle's trail. Head her off before she reaches Dodson." He went into the hut.

Dom took care of the horses.

Gere and Lester smoked, walked to the brush, sat on rocks, and looked up at the sky, darkened now, with stars beginning to emerge.

"What did you think?"

"Of what?"

"Don't be dumb, Lester. How Brome shot Doc."

Lester shrugged. "Brome had a grievance."

"What grievance?"

"The woman. He's loco 'bout Belle."

"Loco, yes. But why'd he kill Doc? They were close in Yuma, too. Doc was the only one he'd trust with Belle.

Then he shoots the man. Why? For being dumb, he says. That's one hell of a reason. Anyone can be dumb, sometime. You or me."

Lester smiled. "Especially you."

Gere's face was hard. "Brome's gone too far."

Lester grinned. "I wouldn't tell him."

"I figger you for a smart duck, Lester. What about Durante?"

Lester looked puzzled.

Gere was impatient. "Why'd he shoot Durante?"

"You saw it. He told him to shoot the kid. He didn't. That's why."

"Just between us, Lester, would *you* shoot the kid?"

Lester's smile was quizzical. "If you knew it was you or the kid, Gere, what would you do?"

"Shoot Brome."

Lester stared. "That's interesting."

"I figger you've got brains, Lester. Why did Brome shoot Durante so quick? Think about it."

"Just tell me."

"He did it because he owed Durante ten thousand dollars. That's why. Pretty hard to collect a debt, if you're dead."

Lester nodded. "I knew that."

"You did. What does it tell you about Brome?"

"It's bad if Brome owes you money."

"That's right. He keeps cutting down the men to keep fattening each share. It's easy for him. He's got the fastest draw I've ever seen. He gave Doc a couple beats before he pulled his gun. That took nerve. And speed."

"Why worry, Gere? We've got our split."

Gere frowned. "What the hell am I talking to you for?

We've got to protect each other. If Brome tells either of us to pull our gun for a showdown, we both pull our guns. It's the only way to stop him. Agreed?"

Jester Lester considered it, then smiled slowly. "I agree. We both pull our guns if he threatens one of us."

They looked toward the hut, and saw Brome standing at the doorway. Gere smiled at him. Brome couldn't possibly have heard them, but he was looking at them strangely.

Something more to worry about.

Patiently, Slocum studied the hut through his field glasses, looking for movement. The tracks of the Brome bunch had led them to that hut, obviously a hideaway, its wood severely beaten by the weather but set among thick brush and shrubs.

Twenty minutes of close scrutiny convinced Slocum the hut was empty. He signaled Tad, who'd been lurking with the horses several hundred yards downhill. Tad mounted up, pulled on the roan behind him, and rode toward Slocum.

"It's empty," Slocum said.

When they reached the hut, Slocum, with his natural caution, kept his gun ready, though he was sure the hut was vacant. He pushed the door open.

Tad sat cross-legged on the beat-up chair outside the hut, waiting, while Slocum studied the signs in the hut and the ground around it.

"They're slippery bastards, aren't they?" Tad said.

Slocum nodded.

"How far ahead d'ya think they are?" Tad stared at the land.

"Four hours. They left this morning. Rode west."

"This morning?" Tad looked cheerful. "We're getting close. So they stopped the night."

"I reckon they kept the woman here," Slocum said. "Her tracks look a day older. Looks like she got away. She took two horses, one not mounted, it has lighter prints. They stayed overnight."

Tad's eyes brightened. "She got away? That's wonderful."

Slocum nodded. "I don't think Brome liked that. Because somebody got shot. There's this new grave."

"That's good, too. Leaves four of them."

Slocum looked at the range of mountains and green stretch of land. "Yup, they've gone west, after Belle."

"Yes. Beautiful Belle. Damn, Slocum, I hate to think what this rotten buzzard Brome would do if he gets her."

Slocum's face was grim. "Even a buzzard won't kill its own. This Brome does."

"What do you mean?"

"Figure it. He leaves the woman with one of his men. The woman escapes. What does Brome do? He shoots the man."

Tad thought about it. "I won't ever sleep easy till Brome is dead."

Slocum gave a short laugh. "He's clever and a killer. It's not going to be easy, Tad. You got to think twice about every move." He rubbed his chin. "If they keep heading west, they'll hit Dodson. She might try to make that town, be safer there."

"I've got one prayer," Tad said. "That if Brome dies, it will be my bullet that does it."

Slocum gazed at the sturdy yearling, his tanned, square face. Tad was fast with a gun, but young in the ways of the wicked. A killer like Brome could eat this kid alive. His own prayer was that if Tad and Brome did get into a draw, he'd be there, too.

It was high noon, a bright day, with a blue sky and billowy white clouds. Slocum figured they'd eat and ride within the hour.

14

Belle rode well into the night before she stopped at high ground to rest the horses. She looked back down the trail, but it was dark and moonless. She examined Doc's saddlebag; it had utensils, some hardtack, jerky, ammunition and, God bless, a derringer. She slipped it into the back pocket of her Levi's. There was no point in taking both horses; it slowed her down.

She couldn't know when Brome had reached the hideaway, but it'd be wise to estimate a few hours after her departure. The big question was, would he track her immediately or wait till daybreak? Tracking at night was not a good idea, especially on a dark night; he might guess she was headed for Dodson, but he had no guarantee. She imagined his men would be saddle sore from all their riding. Yes, she could safely sleep a couple of hours, then go west to Dodson; it was not a law and order town, but she'd be better off than on the trail. Brome would search for her there; she was certain of that. He wouldn't give up his revenge. But she could take a few hours of sleep. She put out Doc's blanket roll and slept restlessly, and when she opened her eyes, there was a glimmer of light on the horizon.

She made coffee, ate hardtack, then put Doc's saddle and saddlebag on her horse. She turned Doc's horse loose. He wandered to some nearby grass and began to graze.

She put her foot in the stirrup, swung onto her horse, and rode west. She rode for three hours steadily, finally stopping at a small stream to let the horse drink. She washed the sweat and grime from her face and body and filled her canteen. Then she built a fire, made coffee, and ate beef jerky. The sun was rising, and the day was warm.

"Your coffee smells good," a voice said.

She jumped a bit. She had heard nothing, but the man stood there, against the brush. He didn't smile. He was hatchet-faced, with deep-set dark eyes, a thin mouth, and dry, pocked skin. His brown hat was crumpled and his gray shirt looked grimy. He wore his holster and gun low.

She had to admit that nothing about him appealed to her, not a man she'd lean on for help against the Brome gang. What grieved her was that he'd been able to get that close so quietly. Clearly, he had known of her camp and left his horse back somewhere while he came up noiselessly. He had all the makings of a drifter. Had he been following her?

"Can I share your coffee?" His voice was flat, toneless.

"Yes, sure."

"D'ya have another cup?"

She wanted to ask about his horse but put that aside. "Help yourself."

"Thanks." He rummaged through the utensils on the ground, took a cup and poured from the coffeepot.

He sipped his cup, holding it in both palms as he watched her.

"I picked up movement," he said. "I thought it might be Injuns. So I left my horse back in the brush and thought I'd look. Didn't expect to find a filly out here. A good-looking filly."

His dark eyes were blank; there was no way to know if he was telling the truth.

"I wondered about your horse," she said, just to say something.

He shrugged. "You never know 'bout Apaches. They'll scalp yuh when you least expect it." He paused. "Surprised me, you traveling alone in these parts." He studied her. "Ain't you 'fraid?"

"Afraid of what?"

"Well, Injuns." Then he grinned widely. "Maybe bandits. Don't seem smart for a good-looking filly to go wanderin' around by herself."

"You think so?"

"Yup." He pushed his scruffy hat back and scratched his head. "Reckon what you need is someone to ride along with you. Sort of take care of you."

"Is that what I need?"

He was silent.

She looked down the trail, wondering how close Brome was. Between this man and Brome, her situation looked lousy.

"Where yuh headed?" he asked.

"Dodson."

He nodded. "I'm goin' there. Might be a good idea to

team up. Hate to think of you runnin' into Apaches. Or outlaws. They could be bad to a filly like you."

"How far to Dodson?" she asked.

"Doncha know?" His eyes gleamed.

"If I knew I wouldn't ask, would I?"

He was silent.

Then he said, "I reckon you're one of them."

She stared at him. "One of what?"

"A smartass, mean filly. That what you are?"

She took a deep breath. "I don't know what I am. But I'm thinking maybe you ought to go about your business, and I'll go about mine."

He just leaned down and poured more coffee into his cup. He gazed at her. "See. I knew it."

"Knew what?"

"That you're a smartass filly. Got a saucy mouth. You cut a man down."

She bit her lip. The man was loco, dangerous. She was running into rattlers, lately; Brome and this loco. How'd you handle him? You couldn't. He'd been following her, probably watched her when she bathed. He had an evil face.

"Maybe we could ride together to Dodson after all," she said.

That stopped him. "You mean it?"

"Sure."

His hatchet face wrinkled as if he was pleased. "I'll tell yuh. Dodson's only five miles west."

"That's nice."

His dark eyes glowed weirdly. "But you can do a lot in five miles."

"Like what?"

His gaze traveled over her body and he took a deep

breath. "Maybe I oughta show you." He stepped toward her.

"Don't you want to get your horse first? You'll need to get your horse if we're goin' to ride."

He paused, perplexed. A look of cunning twisted his features.

"No hurry about that. First things first." He stepped toward her.

"Just a minute. What are you goin' to do?"

He grinned, and his pocked face looked devilish. "What the hell d'ya think? I been followin' you the last five miles. What d'ya s'pose I followed you for?" His teeth showed yellow in an evil grin as he came toward her.

To his surprise, she smiled. "Well, I'm glad you followed me. I was getting mighty lonesome, traveling alone."

He looked astonished. Up to this moment, he'd been thinking she'd be a struggle, that he'd have to knock her a bit to tame her. But he'd been wrong. The filly was lonesome. She was alone, hungry for a man to give it to her, to give her a good time. She was smiling, she held out her arms. Well, he thought, it was a bit disappointing that he couldn't knock her a bit, but it'd be easier this way, he could knock her later. More fun. He looked at her breasts, they were good-sized, and she had fine hips, too. She'd have firm flesh. He went to her, felt her strong, curving body against him. Damn, a fine piece of woman. She squirmed her body, like she was nestling against him. One hungry bitch, wasn't she. Then he felt the cold thing against his left side. He froze, tried to grab it, but he heard the cracking sound, and felt the hot, scalding and tearing on the side of his left chest. Rage streaked through him and he tried to grab her throat, but his arms were suddenly weak; he couldn't raise them. He saw her moving back, saw the derringer in her hand. He saw her staring, then she dimmed, then he saw only blackness. Then he died.

15

Thick rain clouds were starting to drift in from the north, but it didn't worry Brome. What bit at him was the sight of Lester's horse, a dun, which slowly developed a slight limp.

Brome pulled up and the dust swirled when they all stopped.

Gere looked curiously at Brome. "What's up?"

He glared at Gere, then at Lester. "I'll tell yuh what's up. That damn hoss of Lester's is limpin'. That's what's up. And we need that like we need rattlers for lunch."

Lester looked apologetic. "Sorry, Brome. Hosses get lame."

Brome wrinkled his nose as if smelling something bad. "Why's it always happen to you?"

"What happens to me?" Lester looked aggrieved.

"Trouble," Brome said irritably. A lame horse meant a slowdown, the worst thing when tracking Belle.

He glared at the dun, her head low, weary of running on a hurting foreleg. "Maybe we oughta shoot the damned hoss and put you behind Dom."

Lester stared at Brome. "You'll have to shoot me first."

Brome smiled slowly. "Not a bad idea." He looked at the other men; they were not smiling.

"Yeah, why don't we shoot Lester and split his take?" said Gere, his eyes stony.

Brome's jaw hardened. "Don't get smart, Gere. I meant it as a joke."

"Not easy to tell when you're joking, Brome."

Brome looked up at the gathering rain clouds and frowned. "Gere, you're a tough hombre, you got guts. It took nerve to say that. I like nerve in a man. I'll let you get by with that remark. But don't make another."

Gere's eyes blanked.

Brome stared at him. "What's in your mind, Gere? Spit it out. I don't like riding with a man with a grievance."

Gere felt on dangerous ground. Brome could suddenly decide to go for his gun and he couldn't match Brome's fast draw. But there also was the danger that in the end, Brome could pick them off, one at a time. Best to clear it now while he had Lester and Dom for support.

"Okay, Brome, let's talk. Tell us, why'd you shoot Durante? The guy sprung us from Yuma. We'd still be rotting there, if not for him."

Brome was silent a full minute. "So that's what's stickin' in your craw, Gere? I'll tell you. I grieved about Durante. But not for long. Durante didn't break us out because he was bighearted. Did it for money. Trouble is he was greedy. I offered him five thousand, he squeezed me for ten. He had me by the balls. That was one mark against him. I don't hit a man for one mark." His voice went silky. "But the second came when he wouldn't shoot at Selby's. That's why I shot him."

He paused to light a cigar and stared at the men. "You guys are running for me. I got you outta Yuma. You wouldn't be running free if not for me. I expect you boys to do what I ask. That's the setup. If you don't want that setup, you can take a ride." He paused. "But I wouldn't like it."

Gere was silent. The threat was clear; if you rode, he'd pull his gun. They'd had to ride under his conditions. But Gere was far from happy with Brome's explanation. Brome had shot Doc, too. Why? Because he screwed up. There'd always be a reason to shoot, but the bottom line was this: It paid to shoot a man and split his loot.

Brome flipped his cigar, watched it swirl in the air and hit the ground. "Look. We're a gang; we need each other. There's plenty of guns out there looking for us. Let's not make it easy for them, quarreling. What we need to think about is Lester. His horse is lame. He needs another."

Dom spoke up. "There's the Laurel station some miles north of here. The stagecoach stops there for fresh horses. We might get one for Lester there."

"There's an idea," said Brome. "We'll borrow one horse. Pay 'em if we can. If not, take it. Belle won't get away. She got two places to go—Twin Forks or Dodson."

Brome looked at Gere. "I hope we cleared the air. I hope nuthin's eatin' your guts. I once heard Jesse say, 'A gang is good as its weakest link.' I reckon he ought to know—he lasted a long time. What killed him was treachery. He was backstabbed by one of his own men." Brome's smile was icy. "There's a lesson in that. What d'ya s'pose it is, Gere?"

Gere was amused. "Never turn your back on a friend."

Brome laughed. "That's right, Gere. It's why I try to ride only with loyal men."

They rode north and by late afternoon the stage station came into sight. Brome studied the layout: a corral with four horses, replacement for the Laurel stagecoach, and a small station where the travelers, four men with light baggage and two brawny Wells Fargo men, were perched on chairs in the shade, their legs on the railing, one chewing tobacco and whittling wood.

The approach of the four riders piqued their interest, for the two Fargo men sat straight and put their feet on the ground.

Brome smiled: his men were tough-looking hombres, not the kind to give you peace of mind. They rode up in a cloud of dust. Brome came off first from his saddle.

"Howdy," he said.

The whittling man put down the wood and stuck the knife in his belt. He nodded pleasantly. "Grady's the name, mister. What can we do for you?"

"Grady, that's real polite. We've got a lame horse. We'd like to buy one of yours."

Grady's eyes narrowed. "Well, mister, I wish I could oblige you, but these are fresh horses we keep for the stage. It's due in an hour."

Brome nodded. "I realize that, Grady. We're lawmen on the trail of an outlaw who shot a coupla cowboys back in Aurora."

"That so?" Grady smiled like he didn't believe a word. "Sure wish I could do it. But the company would burn my ass. I can't do it."

Brome stopped smiling. "We need the hoss real bad. We'll give you fifty dollars for that brown mare, and leave the lame hoss."

Grady's light blue eyes looked at Brome, at his broad-boned face, small pitted eyes, hefty shoulders, his smooth-handled Colt. The three men riding with Brome had gone to the station to wait in the shade.

He spoke softly. "Mister, I'd like to oblige you. That's a fancy price for the hoss, and I 'preciate it, but the company hired me because they figured I'd not break their rules. We got to keep a tight schedule for the stage; our passengers depend on it."

One of the men, waiting for the stage, sitting in the shade with the other travelers, had been listening hard; now he sauntered forward. He was dark-haired, with intense eyes, thick brows, and a thin nose in a oval face.

"What's the trouble, Grady?" His voice was hard, and his look at Brome was cold, searching.

"Well, Johnny O," said Grady. "This gent has a lame hoss. Says he's chasing an outlaw. I told him the company is strict. We don't trade our hosses."

"That's right, mister." Johnny's tone was cool, as if he didn't think much of Brome and didn't care if he knew it. "The stagecoach has a schedule. You can't grab a hoss and leave the passengers sitting on their asses, just waitin'."

Brome's gray eyes stared at Johnny, a professional gun-man, maybe worse. He'd met men like that, who just by talking, beat you down. He didn't take it kindly. But Brome didn't want a fuss. He ignored Johnny O and turned to Grady. "We need a horse. Give you a hundred dollars for the brown mare."

"The horse is not for sale," said Johnny O.

"Who the hell invited you into this discussion?" Brome's voice was icy.

Johnny's face hardened. He was a good-looking hombre, built sinewy. He looked fast and dangerous. "I don't aim to sweat in this hot sun because you need one of these horses." He peered sharply at Brome. "You look mighty familiar, mister. Have I seen you somewhere?"

Brome's lips twisted ironically. "Depends where you've been."

Johnny O stroked his chin. "It's nowhere I been. It's a picture I'm thinkin of, mister. Picture of a wanted man."

Brome's nostrils widened. It was as he suspected, this Johnny son of a bitch was a bounty hunter. Since his escape from Yuma, they probably had a poster out plastered around. But why tangle with this pesky polecat? It would slow them down. Brome wanted a horse and to get back on Belle's trail.

Again he turned to Grady. Maybe if he raised the ante, he'd get the horse. "I told you, Grady, I need a horse real bad. I'll give you two hundred dollars."

Johnny O's face set suddenly. "Got plenty of money, ain't you? What's your handle, mister?"

Brome turned slowly back to him, his voice silky, "Can I give you some advice, Johnny O? If you stick to your business, you'll live a lot longer."

Johnny's dark eyes were glowing, everything about him, Brome could tell, was keyed up.

"Mister, I'm stickin' to my business. And it tells me you're Brome—bank robber and killer—your carcass is worth a thousand dollars in Aurora."

Brome watched him slip into the gunfighter's crouch.

"Now," said Johnny O, "you're worth it dead or alive. How do you want me to collect it?"

"You're just goin' to collect six feet of dirt," grated Brome.

In the hot sun they stood looking at each other, while Grady backed away. The others, from a distance, stared.

The silence was overpowering; then both men went for their guns. Grady, watching Brome, saw a blur as his hand moved for his holster. He heard two shots, but the second, from Johnny O, went wild as Brome's bullet hit his chest. He stumbled back two steps, put his hand to his chest, gazed at the blood, then looked puzzled at Brome, as if something had happened he couldn't even dream of. The idea that he'd been beat reached his mind, and he fell. He lay there, breathing laboriously. Then he stopped breathing.

The spectators had watched, hypnotized. Johnny O, bounty hunter, had brought many outlaws to justice. Finally he had met the gun faster than his own.

Brome turned, his gun pointing. "Reckon I'm goin' to take that brown hoss after all. I wanted to do it legal, but it's too late now. Just throw your guns, gents."

Brome's men had been watching from the station. They never expected Brome to have trouble.

Grady watched them switch the saddle from the lame dun to the brown mare. They looked back once before they rode off.

"That's the fastest gun I ever seen drawed," Grady said to the other Wells Fargo man.

"Now we have a horse. Let's ride," said Brome.

Ride they did, but twenty minutes later the heavy clouds broke and rain crashed down on the dry earth. They found shelter under an overhanging crag. By the time the sun came out, the tracks had been wiped out everywhere. Brome's face was dark. The men looked at him.

"There's two places she could go," he said. "Twin Forks or Dodson. We'll split. Me and Lester to Twin Forks. I figger she'll go there, 'cause she expects us to go to Dodson. If she's not in Twin Forks, we all meet in Dodson."

"What do we do if she's in Dodson?" asked Gere.

"Nothing. If she tries to leave, one of you go after her." He smiled viciously. "Nail her. Do whatever you have to do. Got it?"

They nodded.

Gere and Dom started toward Dodson.

Brome watched them. "Okay, Lester. Let's go find pretty little Belle. I get a burn in my gut every time I think of her. I know only one way to put that out."

It was late afternoon when Slocum noted with surprise that Brome's tracks turned north.

In the distance was a long stretch of dry, parched land. The broad-shouldered mountains stretched west, and above them was a sky heavy with clouds.

Slocum rubbed his chin. "Wonder where he's headed? I thought he was going to Dodson." He studied the tracks, then turned to Tad. "One of the horses has gone lame. Should slow them down. Rain won't do us much good. Let's get moving."

He soon realized that Brome's destination was the Wells Fargo station. He's probably going there for a fresh horse, he thought.

Brome had taken the stagecoach trail, which enabled Slocum and Tad to pick up time. They reached the Wells Fargo station where two men had just finished doing a burial.

Slocum and Tad watched one man smooth dirt over the

grave. They rode up to him and dismounted. The brawny man stopped, leaned on the shovel, and looked at them.

"Who was it?" asked Slocum.

"A bounty hunter called Johnny O. Fastest gun around here, but not fast enough."

Slocum looked grim. "What happened?"

"Damned outlaw came in with a lame hoss, wanted one of ours. I said we couldn't do it. Johnny recognized him from a poster. I never figured Johnny'd lose the draw. But he did."

"Brome?"

Grady put the shovel down, reached into his pocket for a tobacco chew. "That was him. Brome. Mean hombre." He looked curiously at Slocum and Tad. "What's your deal?"

"We want him, too."

Grady looked doubtful. "Well, you'd best be careful. He's got the fastest draw I ever seen."

Slocum looked at the passengers waiting in the station. "So he came to trade his lame hoss? Seems you had a chance to stop him, all those men."

"Our passengers? They wanted no part of it. But how d'ya stop a man like that? An outlaw. And he had three tough buzzards with him. No, you don't stop a man like that, he'd shoot you quick as look at you." Grady glanced at the corral. "I'm goin' to catch hell from Wells Fargo. When the stagecoach comes in, I've got a lame horse."

Slocum looked at Tad, then at the sky cluttered with heavy rain clouds. There'd be a big downpour within the hour and it'd wipe out the tracks. What to do?

Brome had been riding west toward Dodson before the horse went lame. Dodson was a good bet for Brome and his polecats. In a town like that, desperadoes thrived.

"Let's go to Dodson," he said to Tad. "Got a feeling we'll get a smell of him there."

"Maybe we'll get a showdown in Dodson," Tad said hopefully. "Can't keep ridin' forever."

Grady watched them ride, a man and a boy after a deadly outlaw and his bunch. The man must be loco, he thought.

16

It was late afternoon when Slocum and Tad reached Dodson and the sky was fiery, streaked with crimson and orange.

They walked their horses down Main Street where Slocum saw a fracas in front of the saloon. Two cowboys, facing each other, were charged up like fighting cocks, talking mean. Then came a sudden silence, and the onlookers started to back away. Slocum quickly turned to Tad. "Move out of the line of fire." They slipped off their horses and eased to the side of the livery.

Clearly, fiery words, too late to withdraw, had been said between the cowboys. There was the deadly silence that precedes a showdown. The two cowboys were frozen, crouched; then they grabbed at their holsters. Both fired at the same time. Both staggered back, went down sprawling, and lay on the ground.

The crowd surged forward, looked at them bleeding. "Get 'em to Dr. Rollins, quick," someone said.

The young men were carefully picked up, loaded on a wagon, and driven off. The crowd milled around; some went back into the saloon.

"A red-hot town," Slocum said.

"Yeah," said Tad. He was depressed by the sight of the wounded young men, but his mind soon focused on what brought them to town. He looked searchingly at the men dawdling outside the saloon, and near the cafe. He didn't know what Brome or anyone in his bunch looked like. He was looking for four tough men.

The sight of the wounded young men had bothered Slocum. He felt it was a bad omen for Tad. He didn't want Tad barreling into the saloon and going off half-cocked, in case the bunch was there.

"Hey, Tad," said Slocum. "Whyn't you mosey over to the general store? We need jerky, coffee, beans, and bullets. After that, go to the hotel, get us something for the night. It'll feel good to sleep in a real bed for a change."

Tad scowled, wondering what Slocum had in mind. "And what are you doin'?"

"I'll mosey around, just looking. Don't worry, I won't do anything unless you're there. After you finish, drop into the saloon." By that time, Slocum felt, maybe things would be clear.

Slocum watched Tad go toward the general store and the hotel; then he started for the saloon.

It was big, called Last Chance, with a mirror behind the bar, a spacious area for poker and faro games. There was plenty of drinking, laughing, and smoking. Slocum found a space beside a curly, dark-haired cowboy. The barman, who they called Bronc, came over, poured whiskey for Slocum and left the bottle.

Slocum looked at the drinking men in the saloon, a motley crew. He lifted his glass and muttered to the rugged cowboy sitting next to him at the bar. "Helluva town."

"Yeah."

"Shoot in a crowd like this, you'd hit three outlaws," Slocum said, smiling.

The hombre didn't smile.

Slocum looked at him. He had a strong face, sharp nose, curly hair; his wide-spaced dark eyes were a bit fuzzy from drink. He looked quick, unpredictable. It might be hard to guess his next move.

Slocum smiled easily. "Wouldn't surprise me if *you* were an outlaw."

The hombre turned to stare with his blurred eyes. He picked up his drink, tossed it off, and made a face. "Whiskey ain't much." He glowered at Bronc who was standing near. "This is mule piss."

"Don't like the whiskey, don't drink it," Bronc replied.

Anger slowly appeared in the hombre's eyes, then he shrugged. "Rotten whiskey is better than none."

Slocum looked at the crowd in the saloon. He studied each man but found none that fitted Brome's description. Had he lost Brome?

Slocum felt flat out. Brome wasn't here.

Though the rain had wiped out the tracks, he had figured Brome would land in Dodson. Did he veer off to Twin Forks instead? But that was a small town, not the sort Belle would go to with Brome hunting her. Though Dodson was bigger, it was no great town for law. There were plenty of towns like this, with tough characters, where desperadoes felt easy, where the law was loose. Brome would hit Dodson sooner or later, it was his kind of town.

Well, he, Slocum, would take it easy. He was saddle sore from miles of riding, and a bed and roof would be welcome. And the ladies in the saloon wore dresses that showed sexy flesh, nice to look at.

Slocum looked at one, curvy and cute, with tangled strawberry blonde hair. She seemed busy talking to a drunken cowboy. Slocum smiled, remembering the saloon tart who once told him, "A drunken cowboy is ready to screw like a rabbit, but his pecker is dead lead."

"You just ride in?" asked the hombre next to him, trying to focus his fuzzy dark eyes on the stranger.

Slocum shrugged. "Been here a while." He didn't like direct questions. In a bar you didn't know what nut you were talking to. In his time, he'd met some crazies who, fired with booze, would pull their guns because you sneezed at them.

"What was that fight about?" Slocum asked.

"About nothing," the hombre said.

"How do you know?"

"It's always about nothing."

Slocum smiled. The hombre was a philosopher. He looked over at the woman, still talking to the drunk cowboy.

He turned to the hombre. "Where you ridin' in from?"

"I don't know," the hombre said.

Slocum smiled. He had enough whiskey to be insolent, but not enough to be insulting. "Sorry to bother you."

Then the hombre said, "I'm lookin' for a filly. Maybe you seen her."

Slocum raised his glass and drank, then looked at the hombre. "Yeah, what's she look like?" He considered the possibility that this might be one of Brome's boys, looking for Belle. Brome could be nearby.

"Look like?" the hombre drawled. "Pretty. Blonde hair. Beautiful piece. Sexy. Know what I mean?"

"Reckon I know what a sexy filly looks like," Slocum said, eyeing the strawberry blonde across the room.

"Seen her?"

"I've seen plenty of them. Sexy fillies."

"This one's blue-eyed, built. You'd look at her."

"Yeah, I seen a woman like that."

"Where?"

"Right there, on the other side of the saloon."

The hombre stared at him. "She ain't goin' to be *here*. She ain't a slut."

Slocum smiled. "Why the hell are *you* lookin' for her then?"

The hombre didn't know whether to smile or be insulted. He just raised his whiskey and drank.

"What's your handle?" Slocum asked.

"Dom."

"I'm Slocum. Tell me more what she looks like."

"What the hell. She's a hunk of woman. You see her, you want to screw her."

"That right? Well, I've seen fourteen women like that since I hit town."

Dom looked at him and shook his head. "She's got blue eyes, she's saucy, she's wearing Levi's. She's a piece. Name of Belle."

"Seems like I saw someone like that riding down the street."

Dom looked happy. "Wouldn't surprise me if she's here." He lifted his drink, poured another from the bottle.

"Ain't you goin' after her?"

"Naw. She won't go anywhere. Just so she's in town."

"What'd she do to you?"

"Didn't do anything to me. I've got a sidekick who's mighty interested."

"Who's your sidekick?"

Dom turned to look at him, dimly aware he might have been talking too much to this stranger. "What's your trouble?"

"What d'ya mean?"

"You're damned nosy. Keep askin' questions." Dom leaned forward. "A curious cat put his nose in a mousetrap and bam! Know what I mean?" He grinned widely.

"No, I don't."

Dom had been drinking steadily for hours, and his usually acute mind wasn't working.

"You come in here and ask a lotta questions. I knew a man who asked a lot of questions. Then he couldn't talk anymore."

"Why?" Slocum smiled.

"He asked one question too much."

Slocum smiled. "Wouldn't be surprised if you're ready to pull your gun. About nothing."

Dom considered it. "Yeah, it would be nuthin'. Well, mister, it's been good talkin' to you. I forget why." He got up and walked unsteadily toward the poker game.

Slocum watched him. Dom stopped behind a tough looking polecat sitting in the game. He wondered who the man was. He didn't fit Stiller's description of Brome.

Again, Slocum thought of Tad and wondered what had slowed him down. By this time, he should be finished with his chores. Tad wanted to be in the action, and that should have brought him double-quick to the saloon.

Slocum's impulse was to mosey over to the poker game and find out about the player who Dom was standing behind. Perhaps he'd wait a bit longer for Tad; he poured himself another drink.

After Tad left Slocum, he walked to the hotel where he reserved rooms for the night. Then he sauntered down the street, looking at passersby, hoping to spot four tough characters in a bunch. Slocum, who had only a description from the banker, had given Tad a vague idea what Brome looked like. Tad had an eye out for a sinewy man in a yellow vest. But nobody excited his suspicion, and he finally entered the general merchandise store. There were five customers and when one of them, a woman, turned, Tad was jolted. She, too, looked startled.

"Tad Selby, is it you?"

"It's me, Belle."

Belle looked at Tad and her eyes misted with feeling. He looked much like his father, a man she had once cared for. It put her in mind of her tranquil life on the ranch with MacKay, before Brome and his violence exploded in her living room.

Tad, too, felt shock. He had always adored Belle. She'd always been kind to him on visits, and she was his idea of a beautiful woman.

When Tad discovered that the outlaws had grabbed Belle, it horrified him. His boyish imagination pictured the terrible things that Brome and his men could do to the beautiful Belle. Tad's hate for them almost choked him.

Belle came toward him and, in a burst of feeling, clasped him to her breast. It embarrassed Tad, but sent a surge through him.

Others were looking, so he pulled away and gulped for air. He couldn't help but be aware of her womanly body, even while he recognized that her embrace was motherly.

"What are you doin' here?" she asked.

Tad took a deep breath. "Brome shot my father and my brother."

She nodded silently and pressed his hand. Brome had told her he had shot Selby. She felt for him. Tad looked different, more grown-up, like he'd gone through fire, the kind that either destroyed you or hardened you like steel. She liked the strong look of him.

"We're trackin' him. Him and his bunch."

"We? You've got a posse?" she asked hopefully.

"No, it's Slocum and me."

"Who is Slocum?" Her voice was flat.

Tad's eyes glowed. "He's fast. He came to visit dad, and I shot at him, thinking he was one of the killers. But he's father's friend. They came from the same hometown in Georgia. Dad thought a lot of him."

"There's just you two?" She seemed disappointed.

He nodded.

She lowered her head. Not too encouraging. Brome, one of the worst killers in the territory, backed by his tough bunch, against this man and this boy. Not too good.

"Slocum's at the saloon," Tad said. "Sizing up things."

She spoke in a low voice. "I'm sure Brome has been tracking me, but he's not in town. I haven't seen him. Not yet."

"What kind of a sheriff they got?" Tad asked.

"They had one yesterday. He's shot. Sheriffs don't last in Dodson."

Tad was thoughtful. "I'm going to the saloon. To see what's what. You might go to the cafe. Stay there. If nothing's happening at the saloon, I'll bring Slocum. You've got to stick with us from now on."

17

Slocum, tired of waiting for Tad, walked over to the poker game. Four men were playing and five watching. Slocum, too, watched the play, and more particularly, the brawny man called Gere. A narrow-boned face, a glint of humor in blue eyes, sparse black hair combed straight back. He had a big money pile in front of him. He played smart, staring at his opponent before the bet, to read if he was bluffing.

Dom, standing behind him, looked unsteady, itchy. When a pot was finished, he spoke. "Hey Gere, how long you aim to stick in this game?"

Gere grinned. "Long as these boys are willing to give me their money."

"Mebbe you're gettin' rich, but I'm gettin' tired," Dom grumbled.

"Then go lie down. We've got nothing to do but wait,

anyway." He looked at his money pile. "Be dumb to leave when these boys are givin' me money."

"Ain't much fun here."

"Then go lie down, Dom."

Slocum watched Dom scowl, bring his head erect, turn to the door, and walk out, swinging his right arm.

Slocum stroked his jaw. Dom was not his idea of a ruthless killer, but Slocum figured if he was in the Brome bunch, he had to be part of the massacre at Selby's.

One player, irritated with losing, and even more with Gere's boasting, spoke up. "Hey, Gere, why don't you stop blowing your horn and play cards."

Gere smiled grimly. "The less you play, Rafe, the more you save. Because you're the lousiest poker player I ever met."

Rafe scowled, considering what to do. "If you didn't have a lot of money, I'd put a bullet up your ass. But I won't." He turned to the others, smiling. "Don't want the boys to think me a sore loser."

The men laughed.

Gere thought about Rafe's insolence. "You're lucky. I just decided it'd be dumb to plug you, Rafe. Why shoot the goose who lays golden eggs? You jest keep playing and I'll keep winning your money. Can't think of a better deal."

Rafe's face hardened, but he forced a laugh. "All right. Let's play poker and forget the guns. I figger there'll always be time to put a bullet up your tail."

One player stood up and stretched. "Speakin' of time, I've just run out. Gotta get back to my ranch. Got a long ride."

There was a silence, then Slocum spoke up. "Be glad to sit in, if nobody has objections."

The players looked at him. Gere shrugged. "I don't care who sits in. Just warning you, I'm on a streak, and you're putting your money at risk."

Slocum nodded. "One thing I learned, mister, luck is a fickle lady. And no winning streak lasts forever."

Rafe smiled at the lean, green-eyed stranger. "That's my sentiments, friend. Maybe we'll break down this hombre's luck."

Gere gave the stranger a shrewd look. "What's the handle?"

"Slocum."

Gere frowned. Something about this player didn't seem easy to read. He had a lean, fast look, and you couldn't know what was behind his green eyes. Gere felt a streak of doubt and wondered if this son of a bitch, Slocum, might screw up the flow of good cards he'd been getting.

They started to play again, and when Gere drew a king and got one in the hole, he felt Lady Luck was still his sweetheart. Rafe showed queens, Slocum a pair of eights. Since Gere's second king was not visible, he let Rafe push the betting. Everyone stayed. The pot began to build, which Rafe found nerve-racking. Rafe could see only one king for Gere, who bluffed for the fun of it, often winning pots. He felt Gere was doing it again. Slocum had only a pair of eights showing. Gere felt he had the table beat and bet hard. For some reason, Slocum stayed with them as they raised each other. In the showdown, Gere grinned and turned up his hole king, which beat Rafe. "My luck's not changing," he said, reaching for the pot.

"Hold it." Slocum showed an eight in the hole and his three eights won, which jolted Gere.

Rafe grinned as he watched Slocum scoop the pot. "Maybe Lady Luck's taken a walk, Gere," he said.

Gere studied Slocum. "You came in mighty quiet for three eights."

Slocum shrugged. "You boys were kicking it up. I just went along."

"Where you from, Slocum?" asked Gere during the shuffle.

"Five Spots." Slocum looked Gere in the eye, and damned if he didn't see a flicker. "Ever been there, Gere?"

"I been to a lot of places," Gere said.

"Well, if you been to Five Spots recently, you'd know."

"Why?" asked Rafe.

"We had a bad killing. Some thief came down on Bill Selby. Killed him bad. Then shot his kid. Five years old. That was some thief."

Gere stared at his cards.

Slocum glanced around the table. "What do you think of a thing like that?"

"Scum," said Rafe. "There's scum in the world, Slocum."

Slocum shook his head. "Never heard anything like it. A beautiful kid." He turned. "What do you think, Gere?"

Gere scowled. "What the hell are you asking me for?"

"Just making conversation." Slocum stared into Gere's clouded eyes.

Gere's face was as dark as thunderclouds. "We're playing cards, Slocum. We're not in Five Spots."

"Ever been to Five Spots, Gere?"

Gere's voice was cold. "I believe you asked that."

"Yeah, but you didn't answer."

Gere looked at Rafe, then at Slocum. "I came to play cards, not to tell the time of day."

Rafe's face was grim. "You talk like a man with something on his conscience, Gere. Maybe you were in Five Spots, after all."

There was a long silence, then Gere gritted. "I figger you're bored with two things, Rafe."

"Like what?"

"One, bored with this game."

"Could be. What's the other?"

"Bored with living."

Rafe slowly grinned. "Tell you what, Gere. You been talkin' like a fireball. We'll see how good you are. You've got a sack of money." He put a stack of double eagles on the table. "We pull our guns. Winner takes all. Quicker than poker."

Gere studied him, looked at the money, then stood up slowly. "That's a deal."

"Don't do it," said Slocum. "I started this. I feel responsible."

"Just stay out of it," said Gere.

"I've been wanting to do it for the last hour," Rafe said, standing up.

Everyone went fast to the side of the saloon. Slocum didn't like it; he had wanted to squeeze Gere, find out about Brome. But fate stepped in and things had gone haywire. He stood against the wall.

Gere and Rafe watched each other like hawks. The saloon was silent as death. It always went silent for gunfights.

They grabbed at their guns and there were two shots. But only one hit. Rafe catapulted back and fell. He'd been hit on the right side, not a fatal wound, but he lay there, surprised, his face twisted.

"Get him to Dr. Rollins," said Bronc, and three men lifted Rafe carefully and carried him out of the saloon.

Gere gathered the money on the table and put it in his pockets. When the players, including Slocum, came forward, Gere said, "Spoils your mood for play."

Slocum frowned. "I'm sorry to hear that. I was hoping to put a dent in your money bag."

Gere gave him an unfriendly look. "I'll be around, mister. Just bring cash." As he sauntered out the batwing doors he passed Tad who, looking for Brome, closely scrutinized Gere, the blue eyes in the pale face, the brawny shoulders.

Tad walked past the game area and noticed the blood still on the floor. "What happened?" he asked Slocum as they sat at a table next to the wall.

"Cowboy called Rafe got shot by one of Brome's boys. Name of Gere. That's the critter who just passed you."

"Gere!" Tad's eyes blazed. "One of Brome's boys. Why didn't you shoot the hell out of him?"

"Not the right time."

"Anytime's the right time, Slocum."

"I think there's a right time, Tad. There's another Brome man in town called Dom. Brome's not here. Reckon they're waiting for him."

Tad frowned. "Where is Brome? Why didn't they all come to Dodson?"

Slocum looked thoughtful. "I figure they split because of the rain. It wiped out Belle's tracks. They didn't know where she went. So maybe Brome went to Twin Forks, while Dom and Gere came here."

"I know where she went, Slocum. She's here, in Dodson."

Slocum looked surprised. "You've seen her?"

"Bumped into her at the general store. Now she's at Louisa's Cafe, waitin' for us."

"What'd she say?"

"Didn't talk much. I wanted to get here, just in case. Too bad I didn't find out about Gere."

Slocum told himself it was good that he had diverted Tad. He might have gone off half-cocked. "Gere is fast. Be careful. Now let's go talk to her. She may know a few things. Like why the hell the Brome bunch shot your dad and MacKay."

They walked down the street crowded with wagons, horses, cowboys, shoppers, and motley ragtag. The sky over the houses was still in flames, as the sun sank behind the distant mountains.

Belle, sitting at a corner table drinking coffee, was feeling a bit down. She knew Brome was a vicious killer who felt wronged by Selby and MacKay. And her. He had destroyed them, and intended to destroy her, too. What did Doc say? Brome might not kill her, but he'd kill something inside her. She knew what that meant. When she escaped from the hut, her hopes rose. Though she felt more secure in Dodson, it was still a desperado's town, where the gun was the law. And Brome's gun was fast.

The sight of Tad in the store, a familiar face, had heartened her, but he was just a yearling. It was almost comic to think that he had been tracking Brome and his bunch. And with the help of just one man. It was foolish bravado. Brome was deadly.

But now, as Tad led Slocum toward her table, her spirits lifted. He was lean and strong, with a rugged face tanned like saddle leather, piercing green eyes that looked like they never shone with fear. You didn't get a face like that unless you earned it.

She put her hand out.

The strength of his grip seemed to flow into her, and her forebodings eased.

As for Slocum, he was surprised by her looks. When Tad talked about Belle, Slocum put it down to the ravings of an impressionable stripling. But Belle was an outstanding dish. Rich blonde hair, shining blue eyes, smooth, silky skin, a full, lovely bosom. No wonder Dom, at the bar, awash with whiskey, had said, "You look at her, you want to screw her." Slocum grinned at the memory of Dom mumbling those words.

"So you're Slocum. Were you a friend of Selby's?"

"I knew him in Calhoun County. We were sidekicks in the war. I was passing his place and stopped for a visit. Found him dead."

"The Brome gang," she said mournfully.

"Why'd they do it? Money? Tell us what you know."

She shrugged, looking uncomfortably at Tad. She didn't want him to know about his father, but there was no avoiding it.

"We were all friends in Blue River, six months after the war. They were bad days. The ex-soldiers were desperate; they'd go over the line. We did something, not too legal, but nobody got hurt." She coughed. "People in those days did strange things to survive. Anyway, we divvied the money three ways, then drank to celebrate. I liked Selby. Brome was drunk and went mad jealous, started a crazy fight with Selby, hit him with his gun butt. We hated him. Then Brome, ashamed, drank till he passed out. We left Brome behind that night, with his share.

"Something we learned later: The sheriff and his deputies grabbed Brome in that hut, and he got prison. He believed we squealed and stole his share. So when he escaped, he came with a gang for bloody revenge." She bit her lip with the memory.

Slocum thought about it. "The sheriff was tailing you. Caught up with Brome in the hut. Found a passed-out drunk and lots of money. What stopped him from stealing the money?"

Belle stared. "That must have been what happened."

Tad looked a bit shaken. It was disturbing to discover that his father had done something illegal. He remembered his father as always straight and honest.

Slocum touched Tad's shoulder. "They were desperate times, Tad. Hunger and misery. Good men were forced to do bad things."

"I loved my father," Tad said. "I always will. Brome killed him. He has to pay."

Belle's eyes gleamed. She feared Tad would be a sacrificial lamb; she had to warn him. "Brome is the most dangerous man I ever met. He's shrewd and he's got the quickest gun. He robs banks, ruins posses, he gets away with everything."

"We don't fear him," Tad said stoutly.

"I'd gladly shoot him in the back," she said.

"We'll be careful," Slocum said.

"They are four men, and they're terrible. You're two. You don't have the odds," she said.

Slocum smiled. "Maybe we can cut them down to size."

"What do we do about Belle?" Tad asked Slocum.

"They don't know yet if you're here. But they won't do anything until Brome gets to town."

Tad scowled. "She better stick with us. Otherwise, they could grab her."

"Nobody's grabbing me," Belle said quietly.

No, Slocum didn't think they could; she had steel under the silk.

Slocum looked out the window at a wagon loaded with supplies rumbling past, but he was thinking about Tad. The kid was so charged up that he could make a mistake. There was a small town called Greenville just three miles north. He spoke to Belle. "Wonder if it's a good idea for you to ride to Greenville before Brome gets here. You ride with her, Tad."

"You tryin' to get rid of me?" Tad was glaring. "And do this job yourself?" He shook his head. "You're goin' to need my gun."

Slocum laughed. "Don't I know it." He looked at Belle.

"I'm feared of Brome," she said. "I don't deny it. But I'm not ready to run."

"Well, let's think about it. We don't have to do anything right off."

They went out into the street, still cluttered with wagons, horses, and cowboys. The sun had slipped behind the mountains, and the sky was dark crimson.

Then they saw Gere. He was coming down the street, directly toward them. When he saw Belle, he was jolted. He looked at Slocum and remembered his remarks about Five Spots.

His face was grim as he walked toward them.

18

In the saloon at Twin Forks, Brome was leaning on the bar,
feeling dull anger thinking of Belle.

"She's not in this town," said Lester, standing beside
him.

They'd been looking all day and by this time they knew.

Brome glared at his drink on the stained wood counter.
"She went to Dodson, the little bitch."

"It was a fifty-fifty shot, and you guessed wrong," Lester
said.

"Yeah, I guessed wrong, that's what bites my ass. Dodson
is a rough town, so you'd expect her to come here. Well,
Gere will find her and keep an eye on her."

"Should we ride for Dodson?" Lester looked at Brome.

Brome then sighted the girl, a redheaded tart, across the
room, sitting by herself at a table. He felt a stirring in his
groin. For a moment, he thought that he might save himself
for Belle, then decided he'd take this redhead, and do Belle

later. Lately, when he screwed a saloon tart, he'd imagine it was Belle. He sure had a lust for that lady. When he'd been in prison, he had done terrific things with Belle in his imagination.

"Listen, I'll take that redheaded girl upstairs. When I come down, we'll ride for Dodson."

Lester nodded. He watched Brome go to the redhead, who looked him over, smiled, and stood up. Lester smiled, too. One look at Brome, his sinewy body, all tendons and muscle, told her she'd get a good screw. Lester watched them go upstairs, then leaned back, took his hat off, ran his hand over his bald head. He'd lost his hair young, but didn't care much. He was more interested in money. He felt good. The split from the Aurora swag gave him more money than he'd ever had. He had few complaints. Then he thought of Gere and his warning about Brome, who seemed to like the idea of shooting his sidekicks and splitting their take. Was it true or just Gere's fevered imagination? He wondered why Brome had split him away from Gere, as if he suspected they had gotten too buddy. Brome had an uncanny talent for reading minds. Now he was upstairs, pumping the redhead.

Lester had seen some bad hombres in his time, but Brome was special. He couldn't forget the way he shot that kid at Selby's. A five-year-old, smiling, nice-looking, innocent kid. Brome shot him like he was a pig. Brome was one hard son of a bitch. What did Gere say? If Brome had ordered him to shoot the kid, Gere would have shot Brome. If he could. Brome's speed was dazzling. You almost didn't see his draw, it was a blur. The way to hit men like Brome was in the back. That's how the top outlaws went down. That's how they did Jesse James. Well, an outlaw's life was short and merry. Sometimes not so merry.

Lester drank a couple of shots more; time passed, and he felt mellow.

"Hey, you!"

Lester's meditations came to a screeching halt and he looked at the cowboy in front of him. He had just come into the saloon and taken a place at the bar. Lester had been aware of him, dimly, but didn't take notice; he sensed the cowboy had been looking at him.

"I've seen you before," the cowboy said.

Lester felt his flesh crawl. He didn't care to be recognized; it was always a sticky moment. He stared at the cowboy, chunky, a blunt, coarse face with bright blue eyes. Lester didn't know him from Adam.

"That's nice," he said. "So what?"

"So plenty," the cowboy's voice was loud. "I know where I saw you." A big grin spread over his face. "Been to Aurora lately?"

Lester scowled. This looked like trouble.

"Nope, not me."

The cowboy glared. "Oh, yes you have. I ain't about to forget your face, none of you boys."

"What the hell you talkin' about?" Lester didn't know how to handle it. Should he just shoot the coyote before he opened his big mouth or should he buffalo him?

"Yeah, you hit the bank at Aurora. Four of you. I saw you all as you rode past the livery."

Lester's teeth gritted. "You better be careful, mister. You're talkin' loco. You mighta seen someone who looked like me, but it wasn't me."

"It was you. I remember your red sport shirt, your black hat."

"Hombre," said Lester slowly, "you better be mighty careful of what you say."

The men at the bar started to look at Lester.

"You boys cleaned out the bank in Aurora," said the cowboy.

Lester was alarmed. If he didn't shut the coyote's yowling, he'd be in deep trouble. "I'm warnin' you," he said.

"Warning me? You thievin' dog. I'm doin' the warnin'. We're goin' to put a rope round your neck."

Then Lester heard a cool voice. "Trouble, Lester?" It was Brome, who'd come quietly down the stairs.

Lester felt a surge of relief. "This coyote has been throwin' dirty insults."

Brome stared at the cowboy, who looked ugly.

"Yeah, I saw you, too. In Aurora."

"We just rode in from Dodson," replied Brome, smiling easily.

"Oh, no, it was Aurora," the cowboy said, looking at the other men. "I'm sure of it."

"You called me a liar." Brome's voice was icy. There was a sudden silence in the saloon. "Pull your gun, mister."

"Wait a minute."

"You've got one second."

The cowboy snarled and went for his gun.

Brome's move was a streak and the bullet hit the cowboy in the forehead. He dropped like he'd been hit by a ton of steel, and lay motionless.

Brome held his gun and looked around carefully. The cowboys looked subdued. His draw was frightening. "A man don't like to be called a liar."

Nothing was said, nobody moved, as Brome and Lester went out the door.

• • •

As Gere walked slowly up the street, he looked first at Belle, then at Slocum. So these critters knew each other! No wonder Slocum kept talking Five Spots; he was playing cat and mouse, the bastard. There was Belle, beautiful as ever. He would do nothing now. Brome had said to just keep an eye on her. He would be here soon. And who was that kid with the mean eyes? Might be trouble. And Dom had flopped out, but where?

"Well," Gere said, all merry and bright. "If it isn't Belle. We thought you got lost." His tone was smooth. "A friend is looking for you."

Belle's dark eyes flashed. "Do you have a friend, Gere?"

"Oh, yes, you know him. I'm glad you're lookin' so good." He ignored Slocum and Tad, leaning toward her. "To tell the truth, we worried about you, Belle, on the trail all alone. We worried you might run into a crazy hombre. Glad nothin' bad happened."

She smiled acidly. "Oh, I ran into a crazy hombre."

Gere looked interested. "What happened?"

"He's pushing daisies, isn't that how you'd say it?"

Until now, Gere had been ignoring Slocum and Tad as if they were undeserving of attention. A beardless kid with vicious blue eyes, whose bark looked worse than his bite. But Slocum looked tough. Still, Gere had confidence. He had survived lots of showdowns and it kept him cool in tight spots. Actually, he liked this setup and felt playful.

"Pushin' daisies?" he repeated. "We'll have to tell Brome you're to be handled delicately, like dynamite."

Her lip curled. "Handled? Nobody handles me."

Though Slocum had been studying Gere, he was trying to make up his mind about Tad. He could tell, from the kid's eyes, he was going to draw on Gere, and Slocum wasn't crazy about the idea. He'd seen Gere's quick draw on Rafe. Tad was quick, too, and a showdown would be tight. He didn't know whether to hold Tad off; he was young, could make a mistake. The flicker of an eyelash made the difference between life and death. Tad didn't have the experience and if he was a shade late, that'd be bad, not only for the kid, but for Belle, who'd see it. But Tad needed to do some bloodletting to get rid of the hate that was eating him. Tad was gunning for Brome, too, and if he didn't let Tad have a showdown with Gere, he'd surely want to draw on Brome. Ticklish. He stared hard at Gere, an outlaw in the gang. He had done his share of killings, he'd been with Brome at Selby's house. He was in on it. There had to be a showdown! He thought again of how Tad had pulled his gun. Maybe he could do it. Yes, he'd go with Tad.

Tad's eyes were glowing with hate. This Gere was in the Brome bunch who murdered his father. They had killed Seth, his laughing, joy-loving little brother. Tad was livid.

"You been to Five Spots?" Tad asked.

Gere shrugged. "Been a lot of places."

"With Brome?" Tad's voice was choked.

Gere turned to Tad with interest. "Simmer down, kid. You look itchy for a fight. I don't fight kids."

Tad glared. "But you like to shoot kids. You rotten dogs shot my brother."

Gere scowled. Brother! So that's who this kid was. He didn't like it, but the kid was wearing a gun, and his bullet could kill.

"I didn't kill your brother," he said. "Take it easy."

"Who did?"

"Wasn't me."

"What the hell's the difference?" Tad snarled. "You were there. And my father was killed."

There was silence. Gere's eyes stayed on Tad. "Hey, Slocum, better put a lasso on this kid or he'll have a short life."

Belle, too, suddenly aware that Slocum had moved into the background, looked at him anxiously. She felt dread.

Passersby had stopped, even wagons in the center of the street, aware that something was going to explode.

"Blood for blood," Slocum said.

Gere ground his teeth. "Listen, I get no medals for gunning a kid."

"Billy was a kid, too," said Slocum.

Gere's jaw tightened. "It's on your head, Slocum," and his hand flashed to his gun. Starting a beat behind, Tad fired and it was still a split second ahead of Gere. His bullet hit Gere, who staggered, his face disbelieving. Looking at Tad, he shook his head as if· this was the dumbest thing that ever happened, then he dropped. He put his hand to his side. It was bloody.

A crowd gathered close to look at Gere. Someone said, "Get him to Dr. Rollins." Two men lifted him to a nearby wagon and they drove off.

"God," said Belle.

"Damn, I missed him," Tad said.

Belle scowled. "Missed him? You're lucky to be alive." She turned to Slocum, her face dark with anger. "Why? Why'd you let Tad do it?"

Slocum's green eyes glittered. "Because he needed to do it. And I figured he could."

"You might have been wrong."

"But I wasn't."

Some of the pain in Tad's face was gone. He hadn't felt this good in a long time. "Thanks, Slocum, for not butting in. It helped a lot."

"There's still Brome," Slocum said.

Brome and Lester rode toward Dodson. It was dry country and the sun burned down on the raw-backed mountains. When they reached the top of a sun-baked slope, Brome pulled up. Sweat streaked the dust on his cheek. He untied his bandanna and wiped his face. Dismounting, he pulled his field glasses from his saddlebag and looked through them down the hill. Brome frowned when he saw the five riders coming toward them. He passed the glasses to Lester.

"Who the hell are they?"

"The boys in that saloon. The cowboy was yelling we robbed a bank, remember," Brome said.

Lester frowned. "Coming after us for a hanging party? So do we ride or do we shoot?" Someone told him in prison that Brome was a great long-distance shooter. They said he once hit an Apache a half mile away.

Brome took his Sharps rifle from its saddle holster, a rifle with a mule's kick. He set it on a small tripod, sprawled on his stomach, and looked through the sight. The rider out front was a husky, bearded man. He aimed to hit his shoulder and gently squeezed the trigger. The rider jerked in his saddle and fell. The other riders, bewildered, drew their guns and looked around for the rifleman.

When Brome fired again, the second rider jumped, fell, his horse dragging him. The three riders milled around, shouting, pointing to the slope. They were getting the idea. Brome figured one more shot would clinch it. The rifle jumped, and the third man dropped. There was no cover for the last two riders. They turned their horses, spurred them, riding back, hell-bent for Twin Forks. They had enough of the deadeye bastard who could shoot like the devil.

Lester watched through the field glasses. He grinned. "Running like scared rabbits."

"Reckon they've had enough," Brome said.

They started to ride again toward Dodson.

19

As they walked toward the hotel, Slocum glanced at Tad who was silent and deep in thought.

Tad turned abruptly to them. "I'm goin' to ride."

"Ride where?" asked Slocum.

"Just ride." Tad's jaw was hard.

"We better go with you," said Belle.

Tad's voice had an edge. "No, I'd like to be alone."

Tad sounded a bit off center, like he'd just been hit by the aftereffect of the showdown. After all, Slocum thought, he was still a kid and he'd just put his life on the line against a tough gunman. It was hard. Slocum could feel for him, but why be alone?

Belle felt that something was chewing him, and he wanted to work it out himself, so she said nothing.

"All right," Slocum said. "Don't get in trouble."

"What trouble?"

"I told you, there's another Brome gunman around. Name

of Dom. He doesn't know you. But he'll find out about Gere and come looking for a yearling. Look sharp."

"Dom? What's he like?"

"Black shirt, yellow kerchief, brown eyes, sharp nose, walks with a wide stride, swings his right arm. Always looks ready."

Tad smiled. "I'll keep an eye out."

But after he swung over his horse and rode west out of town, he forgot about Dom. He was thinking of his father, who he admired and loved, who they had gunned down—that Brome gang of killers. Since it happened, he felt as if his blood had been poisoned. He remembered how his father looked in death, tied like a hog and ruined by bullets. They shot him like an animal. And this Gere had been one of them.

Gere didn't want to fight because he was a kid, yet Gere had been there at his father's murder. And Seth. The smiling kid who never hurt anyone. They cut him down. Gere deserved to die like a rotten dog. Yet, at the last moment, when Tad fired, he did not aim to kill. Why? Was he too soft? He couldn't afford that. His family had been destroyed and he had to avenge their deaths. Each thug that died cleaned out his hate, gave him more peace.

Oh, yes, killing was new to him, but it had to be done. The blood of his father and his brother called out from the ground. Tad kept riding under the bright moon pouring light on the trees and the great cliffs and making dark shadows. The earth seemed beautiful in the night, but Tad saw nothing of it. He kept thinking of his revenge.

Standing on the boardwalk near the hotel, Slocum and Belle had watched Tad ride off. In the hotel, Slocum suggested she take the room next to his. "At a time like this, it's best that you be nearby," he said.

They walked upstairs and paused at the door to her room.

"Tad is hurting," she said.

Slocum looked thoughtful. "If you're that young, it hurts when you shoot someone."

She looked away for a moment, then stared hard at him. "I was furious that you let Tad take the showdown with Gere. A boy against a fast gunman. It's like murder. You took a terrible chance, Slocum. Did you do the right thing?"

He came into the room and sat on the chair. "It worried me, Belle, but I've seen Tad. He's fast, very fast—if he can keep his nerve. And he was festering. They killed his kin. His hate would eat him alive. He's the kind who'd have no peace until he paid them in blood. He's feeling easier now."

She was thoughtful. "You guessed right. Yes, he had good reason to shoot."

Slocum looked at her lovely, oval face. "They killed your man, too."

She nodded. "Shot him like a dog. They asked for the money, then shot him. Then they burned the house. I wanted to tear them to pieces."

Her dark eyes glowed with rage. Slocum looked at her sleek skin and full lips. "They carried you off."

She nodded. "Brome always wanted me. He had bad ideas. He was going to use me like a dirty rag. His revenge. I was ready to kill him or kill myself, but I got lucky; I escaped."

"Luck, I wonder how much was luck." She was cold steel and rose petals. Slocum found her appealing and she sensed it.

She looked away, then back at him. "Don't misunderstand. I'm no plaster saint. It's just that I'd rather be dead than let Brome get to me."

Slocum understood. He felt a surge of anger at Brome. For revenge, he was ready to let his men abuse this beautiful woman.

"I need a drink," he said.

"I'll have one, too."

He brought the whiskey bottle back to her room. As they drank, he thought about Selby, how they had hog-tied him, then shot him to pieces. So where in hell was Brome now? If he had gone to Twin Forks, and hadn't found Belle, then he'd be in Dodson tomorrow. One gunman traveled with him, and there was Dom. That made three.

"Brome will be here tomorrow, I figure."

Her eyes darkened. "Yes, I believe it."

"He'll hear about Gere, and come for Tad."

"Yes, I fear for him." She drew a deep breath. "And I fear for myself."

"I'll be here."

She drank the whiskey and felt its warmth. Suddenly she reached over and stroked his cheek. "You've got such a strong face, Slocum." Staring into the depths of his green eyes, she felt a strange thrill of pleasure. "I want to tell you something. When I reached this town, my nerves were bad. I had escaped something terrible. I was still afraid because Brome seemed unbeatable. But when Tad brought you, the fear dropped away. I don't know why. I still think nobody can beat Brome. But there's something about you, Slocum." She smiled. "It's hard to feel fear when you're close by. Maybe it's because you don't feel it."

He smiled at her, and yielding to impulse, she suddenly

leaned over and kissed him. It touched him and he put his hands around her face and his mouth over hers. Her lips were silken, warm; he liked the smell of her. He felt the fire start in his groin. She put her arms around him. They stood up and their bodies pressed tightly together. He felt her bosom. His hand went to her breast, he opened her shirt, slipped his hand over the silky roundness, felt the erect nipple. Her hands stroked his body. Her moves were daring.

They paused for breath, then both quickly stripped. She had a full figure, a slender waist that curved into round, womanly hips. Her legs and thighs were shapely. Her skin was smooth and silken.

She gazed at his male excitement and her eyes glittered.

"Slocum, you're all man."

His lips twisted sardonically. "I wouldn't have it otherwise."

He looked at the crest between her thighs and pulled her to the bed. He felt the gust of desire. His hands were over her breasts, the curve of her hips, her buttocks. She drew him to her and brought her thighs apart. He entered the warmth, looking into her eyes, and saw the torment of pleasure. He moved with slow craft, setting the rhythm, and she responded, until he felt the vibrations, her body stiffening. She shivered and groaned. He kept at it, and the vibrations swept through her again and again. His excitement became so intense that he no longer could restrain himself, and his body catapulted to climax; she smothered a scream of pleasurable anguish.

They lay quietly, resting. He felt the warmth and silk of her skin. A woman is a thing of wonder, he thought. Then he grinned, and guessed she could be thinking that about a man.

When he was ready to leave, and reached the door, she said. "If you handle a gun as well as you make love, Slocum, we'll have nothing to fear from Brome."

He shut the door quietly, and told himself, "Too bad it doesn't work like that."

20

Back in Dodson, Dom came out of the hotel refreshed. He had dozed two hours and, looking out the window, saw a full moon glowing in the night sky. In the distance, the cliffs were silvered, and threw long, dark shadows. It was not very late, he guessed; he could see folks still in the street, some wagons, a couple of loud drunks.

His head felt clearer. He'd go to the saloon and push Gere out of that game and get some grub. He remembered that Gere had been playing winning poker, happy as a colt.

Dom went into the street, bright under the moon and oil lamps. He walked around the town, stretching his legs, looking, just in case Gere had left the saloon.

He walked to the saloon. Gere was not at the card table. He ordered a whiskey. Where in hell was that polecat? His horse was still tied to the rail in front. Did he go upstairs with one of the girls or had he guzzled too much and gone somewhere for shut-eye? But drinking like that wasn't his style. He'd turn up, though you'd think he might have stopped at the hotel and said something.

Dom stood at the bar until he recognized a cowboy who had played poker with Gere. He was sitting with one of the girls. Dom walked over.

"Excuse me," he said politely. "I'm looking for my side-kick, Gere. He was in the game with you. Remember?"

The man stared at him. "Gere. Yeah. So you're lookin' for him?" He glanced at the girl. She just shrugged.

"That's what I said."

"Well, it's goin' to be easy to find your sidekick, mis-ter."

Dom didn't like the man's tone. "Where is he?"

"He's not goin' anywhere. Heard he got shot."

"Shot!" That hit Dom. "Damn it." And Gere was a fast gun. It took a long moment while he digested it. "Dead? Is he dead?"

The man shrugged. "Yeah, heard he was dead."

"Was it a poker fight?"

"Naw. The way I heard it, he had a run-in with a kid on the street. Wonder if it was Billy, because he pulled a fast gun. Just a kid, they said." He looked at Dom's face.

Dom cleared his throat. "What was the fight about?"

"One of those things. Nobody knew. Maybe they bumped each other, started shooting."

Dom swore under his breath. One day you're rich, the next day you're dead. But who in hell would hit Gere? A kid? Out of nowhere? It didn't seem right for an outlaw of Gere's standing to be shot by a kid.

So Gere was gone. Dom began to think. Well, maybe

it wasn't all to the bad. Gere's cut from the Aurora bank robbery was still in his saddlebag. No reason not to claim it; he'd just pick up the horse. He'd suddenly become a rich man.

He went outside and looked at Gere's horse, tied to the railing. His impulse was to go quickly to the saddlebag, but he hung back. He suddenly remembered Brome. Better think on it more. He stood on the boardwalk and put his arm around the building post.

Brome was headed this way, coming for Belle.

Dom realized he didn't yet know if Belle was in town, though he seemed to dimly remember some joker at the bar saying he'd seen her. But how would *he* know Belle?

Maybe he should walk around, keep an eye open for her and collect Gere's money later. Brome was the worry. If Gere was dead, Brome would want his money split. Dom lit a cigarillo. If he was clever, he'd get it all. But it was dangerous to cross Brome; if that hellcat thought you did him dirt, he'd shoot in a second.

Dom scratched his head. What if he picked up Gere's saddlebag and kept riding for the border? All right, but if his trail ever crossed Brome, it'd be sudden death. Strange, but he didn't feel grateful toward Brome even though the polecat had pulled him out of Yuma. Brome was a cold-hearted bastard. Dom recalled how he shot the Selby kid. You didn't do such things. Brome had no heart. How could he be loyal to such a man?

Maybe it was better to stick around and see what would happen. He'd lift Gere's saddlebag, bury the money nearby, then come back for it months later, when it was safe. That was the best idea.

Dom felt lighthearted and started for Gere's horse. That's

when he saw the rider gallop in from the west, go off his saddle with a quick, easy jump and tie his horse to the post near the hotel. Dom kept looking at the rider, not aware of why, until he realized the youth of the rider. His skin tingled; then the kid looked at him. Something in that look snapped Dom alert. This kid shot Gere. And Dom felt that he had shot Gere not by accident, as he had been told. He could tell from the kid's look. That boy had showdown in mind; he was gunning for the Brome gang. He knew something. What he knew, Dom couldn't guess, but this kid had killing on his mind. Why? Who the hell was he? Could he have been tracking them all this time? From where? Aurora? They shot five men in that town. Then they shot the posse. So was this kid a lawman? Too young. But he could be kin to someone who'd been shot. What about Five Spots? That's where they had killed Selby and MacKay. But who would he be?

Did it matter? This kid didn't stumble into Gere, he knew him when they met and had killing in mind. But how'd this boy beat Gere? It must have been a fluke; the kid didn't even shave! Dom could read his face. He had a rage on, but was trying to control himself. Dom tingled. Brome always gunned down trouble before it started. Should he?

What's to worry about? If the kid wanted a gunfight, Dom wouldn't step back. He had done a lot of killing in his time, he knew how to pull a gun. And this brat had killed Gere; Dom had liked Gere.

Tad came toward the cowboy who was wearing the black shirt, the yellow neckerchief. That had flagged Tad down when he came off his horse. Slocum said he'd be wearing a black shirt and yellow kerchief. The polecat was looking at him, too. Why? Because he'd shot Gere, and they told him a yearling did it. Okay, so we know each other. This would be Dom, in the killer Brome gang. They murdered his father, burned his home. He would talk to him. He was sure, but he wanted to make absolutely sure.

He came abreast of the man.

"Howdy," Tad said.

Dom looked at him without speaking. He was astounded that Gere had been beaten by this pip-squeak.

"Have I seen you before?" Tad said. He would move slow, you couldn't go off half-cocked and find out later it was the wrong man.

"How the hell do I know that?" The voice rasped.

"I just wondered. You look like I may have seen you somewhere."

"I don't think so." Dom's tone was rough.

"Why?"

"I'd remember a pink skin mug like yours."

Tad ground his teeth. "You ain't polite."

"Do I have to be?"

"I'm just wondering, mister. Ever been to Five Spots?"

Dom blinked. So that was it. Five Spots. The kid was kin to Selby or MacKay. He'd been tracking them all that way and they never picked it up. And Brome was so damn good at that. But they had always come away clean from all their jobs. It was hard to believe that a pip-squeak like this would come after them. A man like Brome, a man like him.

"Are you Dom?" Tad's voice was quiet.

Dom's lip twisted. "Are you the kid who shot Gere? Tell me how'd you do it, hit him when he wasn't looking?"

Some cowboys passing by stopped to observe an interesting situation.

Tad's eyes were blazing. "You lowlife, you murdered Selby. He was my father."

So, it was like he thought. Dom sneered. "Your father got what he deserved. *He* was the lowlife, he squealed on Brome, cheated him."

"You're a rotten liar."

Dom stared hard. "You're pretty young to die, kid. Run along. I'll forget you said that."

Tad's voice rasped. "Draw, or I'll shoot you like a dog."

Dom's hand started down and Tad's hand was a streak. His gun barked and his bullet smashed Dom in the chest. Dom staggered back, cursed, and tried to bring his gun up to shoot, but fell. The gun fired on the ground.

Tad watched Dom as he squirmed. He muttered something. Tad bent down to listen.

"I hate leavin' all that money," Dom whispered.

Tad watched him die. Then he thought of Brome. The worst of them. The most feared gunfighter.

Tomorrow would be the day.

21

Brome had been at the saloon in Dodson only ten minutes before he discovered that Gere had been hit in a gunfight and that Dom had taken residence in Boot Hill.

Brome was astonished. How did it happen? What in hell was going on?

A gunfighter kid, the barman said. The same gunfighter did the damage, a kid. For one uneasy moment, Brome thought it might be William Bonney, the demon gunman they called Billy the Kid, but he was up in Kansas. No, not Billy.

The barman told Brome that Gere was wounded, not dead, and patched up at Dr. Rollins's place.

Brome lifted his drink, thinking. Now he didn't know if Belle was in town or what else was going on. But he did know that he wasn't grieving about Gere. Gere grumbled too much. He didn't like what happened to Durante or to Selby's kid. Maybe this gunfighter had saved him a bit of trouble. So Dom was gone. Well, there was ten thousand dollars in his saddlebag to pick up and divvy. Brome poured another drink. Things were winding down in the outlaw business. Maybe he didn't need a gang, not for a while. He had plenty of money, didn't need to do thieving or killing. He could live on his money. If he thought about it, the kid did him a favor. There was always a hitch with sidekicks; they knew too much, and if they turned, you caught hell. Like Selby; he'd been a pal who turned, squealed; got him locked up in Yuma. And Belle. He hadn't paid her off yet. She started the fracas, the jealous thing, made him beat the hell out of Selby. And she was in town, she had to be.

He gazed at Lester.

"Any idea about this kid?"

"Don't know, Brome. Can't figger it."

Brome put his glass on the bar. "That kid, whoever he is, has lived long enough. Drink up. We'll go to Gere and find out something."

Lester was in no hurry to move. He felt tired. They'd been driving their horses all morning under a frying sun. By the time they reached Dodson, the horses were ready to drop, and he was drooping, but not Brome, a man of steel. He seemed indestructible. And Lester was a bit nervous. The Brome gang seemed almost wiped out. He remembered they had started from Yuma with Danker, Durante, Gere, Doc, and Dom. Only he was left. Gere was hurt. You couldn't figure the angle with a man like Brome. Gere had told him that Brome liked to shoot his men and split their take. It was a worrisome idea. He never felt he could trust Brome. Whatever Brome did, in the end, it always had one aim; to make him richer. He wondered how long he'd be useful to Brome. Brome could decide in a moment that having a gang was pointless. And he was the kind of critter who'd make sure nobody had a thing that could hurt him—put him in jail, or in a noose. If Brome made such a decision, he'd slip a bullet in a man's hide, quick as a wink. Lester raised his glass. Maybe it was time to ease out. But how?

"You're dawdling, Lester, drink up."

Lester gulped his drink.

They found Gere in the house which Dr. Rollins used as a hospital.

"He's weak. Don't stay too long," the doctor told them.

Gere had a big bandage wrapped around his side. He looked pale from blood loss.

He smiled at Brome. "Son of a bitch kid beat my draw. Still can't figger how."

Brome didn't like the look of him. "Always said you had a rusty draw."

"The kid was fast."

Brome stared at him. "Who is he?"

Gere looked at the tree outside the window. "Selby's older kid."

Brome thought about it. "Yeah, Selby had two kids, one older. How'd he know you?"

"Belle was with them."

Brome's eyes gleamed. "She's here."

"Yeah, with a coyote called Slocum. I figger they'd been trackin' us since we left Five Spots."

Brome was astounded. "Since Five Spots. Damn! And I never picked them up."

Gere turned, and his face twisted with the pain. "Too bad the kid didn't shoot straight, I wouldn't be sufferin'. Be through with it."

"He shot straight at Dom," said Lester grimly.

Gere's eyes widened. "The kid? He got Dom?"

Brome nodded. "Dom's gone. We'll split his take." He smiled brightly. "There's always a little good with the bad, Gere. Remember that." He stood up and hefted his gun belt.

"Where you goin'?"

"I'm goin' to punish this kid, then take care of Belle," said Brome.

Gere, with dim eyes, watched him walk out, followed by Lester, who waved from the door.

Gere sighed and turned to the wall.

They were coming out of the cafe and Belle's eyes widened as she looked up the street. When she stopped, Slocum and Tad glanced at her. "That's Brome," she said.

Two men were coming toward them, and there was no doubt which one was Brome.

Tad felt a shock; it seemed he would know him anywhere. He expected he'd look like this. He felt himself shaking and knew it was both fear and excitement. This was the worst of them all, the most dangerous, the killer. The one Tad had to kill so he could sleep nights, so he could be quiet again.

It was Slocum's first sight of Brome and he stared, measuring him. His body was all sinews and gristle; a body designed for a high speed draw. He'd be a hard man to kill. As Brome came nearer, Slocum could see the broad face under the brown hat, the deep pitted gray eyes. He had a killer's face, if ever a man had one, and Slocum had seen lots of outlaw faces in his time. He glanced at the other man, who looked like he wanted no part of it.

Brome came up and addressed Belle, as if the men

weren't there. His boot scuffed the ground. "I did a lot of running to catch up with you."

"Why waste your time?" she said.

"I don't waste my time." He looked at her eyes, her hair, and her body. "You better come with me." He glanced at the men with a bit of contempt. "I suggest you don't make a fuss. You wouldn't want to damage your friends."

Belle shivered. She hated the sight of him, but suddenly she thought Tad and Slocum would be dead within seconds if she resisted Brome. He was capable of action, incredibly quick and terrible. She could visualize him, his lightning move, shooting twice; she could see the men squirming and dying in agony on the ground. No, she couldn't sacrifice them. She'd go with him, then later kill him or herself.

She turned. "Slocum," she said, "please don't fight. I don't want blood on my head."

Brome's face was grim. "That's smart, Belle. You just get on your horse and ride west, out of town, and wait till I come. Don't try anything." He looked curiously at the kid.

Tad found his voice. He had been astounded at Belle. "Don't move, Belle. Don't do a thing. This rotten killer is going to pay."

Slocum spoke sharply. "Tad! Don't get into this."

Brome turned leisurely to look at Slocum, at the lean, strong face, the piercing green eyes with no look of fear, the powerful body. Brome was a bit impressed, but not much. Brome had never lost a draw, not even near, and he didn't expect it to happen now. "And who the hell are you?"

Slocum smiled slowly. "So you're Brome. I've been trailing you since Five Spots."

"You—and what the hell for?"

"You shot a dear friend, Selby. Shot him like a hog."

"He deserved it, Slocum. He turned on a friend. He put the law on me and stole my money."

Slocum shook his head, his voice was cool. "Selby never turned on a friend in his life. He never touched your money. You're not a very smart hombre. They tell me you're a fast gun, but you're not fast in the head. It never occurred to you that the sheriff stole your money. You were out cold when he got there."

Brome had considered that, but didn't buy it. "And what about the sheriff? How'd he get there, since you know it all?"

"He'd been tracking you, with deputies—from the bank. Why shouldn't he catch up?"

Brome was silent. They had all tried to tell him that, Selby, MacKay, and Belle, and he never bought it, but when Slocum told him, he began to believe it. Had he been wrong all this time? A strange, corroding feeling went through him. Was it regret? He had suffered in prison, and someone had to pay. He had picked on Selby and MacKay because they never went to prison. Then he thought of the smiling kid who he shot to make Selby suffer. Had he been wrong? No, he couldn't be. To hell with it, it was gone, all down the drain.

In the silence, the hot sun burned the dry, wide street, where curious cowboys had stopped to watch what could be a showdown.

Brome's voice grated. "I don't care about it. It don't matter anymore. I want you, Belle. And nobody's going to stop me. I warn you."

"I'm stopping you," said Tad.

"Don't do it," said Slocum.

But it was too late, for Tad had gone for his gun.

Brome's move was dazzling. His bullet shot the gun from Tad's hand.

"I've done enough damage to your kin," Brome said, holstering his Colt. "Get your horse, Belle."

"Stay where you are, Belle," Slocum said.

Brome's deep, pitted eyes watched him. "Mister, I got no fight with you. You can go on livin', or you can die. Choose."

"Let's see who dies," Slocum said.

The street was silent, not a bird flew. The hot sun burned. Everyone was motionless as the two men stared at each other.

Brome went for his gun, his confidence high, his hand moving like a lightning streak. As his hand reached the trigger, he felt the scalding, tearing thing in his flesh. Then he felt empty, like life had left his body. It flickered back, just for a moment, while he realized that this man with the green eyes, out of nowhere, had beat him, and that he'd be dead here, in this jerkwater town filled with nobodies. He looked at them, saw Belle's face, the kid's face, Slocum's face; then he saw the scorched sky. A buzzard was flying overhead. He didn't want to see a buzzard. Then he stopped seeing.

They were saying good-bye. The roan chafed, eager to ride.

"They burned your houses," said Slocum. "After the money's returned to the Aurora bank, there'll be enough left over in those saddlebags for you to build new homes."

Belle kissed him. "If you ever pass through Five Spots, you must stop in and see me. You'll always be welcome."

"Count on it," Slocum said and turned to Tad.

"Brome beat your draw. Keep that in mind, boy. You're not the fastest gun in the territory. Not even cock o' the walk."

He looked at the sturdy, strong stripling who, these last few days, had grown up quickly. Slocum smiled broadly. "No, not cock o' the walk, but you sure got the makin's."

He gave Tad a hug, slipped into the saddle, and the roan started to prance.

They watched Slocum ride till he was a small figure against the horizon.

WESTERNS!

at least a savings of $3.00 each month below the publishers price. Second, there is never any shipping, handling or other hidden charges—Free home delivery. What's more there is no minimum number of books you must buy, you may return any selection for full credit and you can cancel your subscription at any time. A TRUE VALUE!

Mail the coupon below

To start your subscription and receive 2 FREE WESTERNS, fill out the coupon below and mail it today. We'll send your first shipment which includes 2 FREE BOOKS as soon as we receive it.

Mail To:
True Value Home Subscription Services, Inc.   12558
P.O. Box 5235
120 Brighton Road
Clifton, New Jersey 07015-5235

YES! I want to start receiving the very best Westerns being published today. Send me my first shipment of 6 Westerns for me to preview FREE for 10 days. If I decide to keep them, I'll pay for just 4 of the books at the low subscriber price of $2.45 each; a total of $9.80 (a $17.70 value). Then each month I'll receive the 6 newest and best Westerns to preview Free for 10 days. If I'm not satisfied I may return them within 10 days and owe nothing. Otherwise I'll be billed at the special low subscriber rate of $2.45 each; a total of $14.70 (at least a $17.70 value) and save $3.00 off the publishers price. There are never any shipping, handling or other hidden charges. I understand I am under no obligation to purchase any number of books and I can cancel my subscription at any time, no questions asked. In any case the 2 FREE books are mine to keep.

Name _____

Address _____ Apt. # _____

City _____ State_____ Zip _____

Telephone # _____

Signature _____✔_____
            (if under 18 parent or guardian must sign)
                Terms and prices subject to change.
    Orders subject to acceptance by True Value Home Subscription Services, Inc.

OTHER BOOKS BY JAKE LOGAN

WRONG QUESTIONS ARE ANSWERED WITH HOT LEAD!

Danker pushed his chair back slowly. "And now, mister, you jest used up all your questions." He showed his teeth in a vicious grin. "Know why I been telling you all this, mister? 'Cause it don't matter. You'll be dead in less than a minute."

Chairs scraped as the men at the table rushed to the walls.

Danker stood up, but Slocum kept sitting. "Would you mind telling me *why* you all shot my friend?"

"Jest stand up, mister, or I'll hit you where you are," Danker snarled, already in the gunfighter's crouch.

Slocum felt his flesh crawling. He watched Danker's hand snake to his gun, as he went for his own gun. Three shots fired, two bullets crashing into Danker— one to his chest, the other hitting him dead center forehead. He toppled back like a sawed tree, a corpse before he reached the floor. His own bullet had gone into the ceiling.